OLD PINES
and Other Stories

By James Boyd

The University of North Carolina Press

MANUFACTURED IN THE UNITED STATES OF AMERICA BY
THE WILLIAM BYRD PRESS, INC., RICHMOND, VIRGINIA

Acknowledgments

In making this selection of my husband's short stories, reflecting his abiding interest in Southern character and the Southern scene, I wish to acknowledge the help of Richard Walser of the English faculty of North Carolina State College, editor of *North Carolina in the Short Story,* and Paul Green, dramatist, novelist, philosopher, and true friend. Without their generous interest and encouragement this volume might not have been published.

KATHARINE BOYD

Southern Pines
May 1, 1952

Contents

OLD PINES
and Other Stories

Old Pines

OLD man McDonald sat in the house of his ancestors watching his little railroad die. Its wabbling single track left the Great Southern in the town below him and, climbing with laborious eccentricity, passed near the composed and graceful portico and the old man himself, and meandered away through a ragged wilderness toward the vanished glories of an abandoned port. The old man's blunt figure at the base of a slender, quiet column stood out sharp and motionless. He was waiting, with his heavy gold watch in his hand, for the evening train to come by.

When he was young, the ruined scrub-clad hills that he could see to the east had borne a vast pine forest stretching away to the sea—great dark trees, shoulder to shoulder, rising tall and true as masts and then, at the very tops, branching fancifully into Japanese designs. Through this as a boy he had run the rough survey for the right of way, blazing the solemn kings with a hardy impudence of which they took no note until too late, when the logging teams came in, and they tumbled stiffly down in impotent majesty.

In time a clean-cut swath wound its way through the forest, and McDonald set himself to gather a nondescript

Negro gang from the few scattered towns of the district. With them he started to build the railroad to the coast, bossing them himself. They moved with unhurried and jocular ease, but they made the little rusty mules hump their backs in the stump pullers while the scoops gently, but tirelessly, graded the red-streaked sand. As the roadbed took shape, the rails were laid and spiked down by buck niggers in groups of three, swinging alternately, in rhythm, with a coughing grunt at each stroke.

They kept working farther into the forest. The little eddy of movement sank into the unfathomed calm. The clink of sledge and the rattle of singletrees faded at birth into the dark maze. The gang made lean-to camps of pine boughs, and sat close at night in front of a great fire. They had always a fiddle or two, and at the music one of them sometimes stood up, rocking gently, and began to shuffle softly in the dust, the great flat feet sliding delicately in a little circle with magic fascination. Then all at once the rest began to sing, and a song which had come from forests of mangrove and ebony vanished down aisles of cypress and pine.

He camped with them, going home now and then in a handcar. As winter came, their spirits drooped, and they huddled around little fires all day. It did not pay to work then, but in three summers he had put the line through. He owed money on every nail and crosstie and knew he could not raise another penny anywhere. But the job was done, and in time he would make it pay.

So he went back to the white house his father had left him, and from his little office at one end he garnered the harvest of the halcyon turpentine days and watched his earnings, puffing mightily in their corpulence, steam by below his window—seeping hogsheads of tar and barrels of acrid rosin. Eastbound moved rotund drums of tobacco and cotton bales to the seaboard port at the end of the road. But best of all he liked the evenings when the gangs of turpentine niggers rolled in, swinging their legs from the flatcars and singing "Deep River."

He was now a man, self-reliant, but very shy. One day when he had gone down the line to the port and was watching the roustabouts spin the bales along the quay to where a Greenock tramp was nudging the piles, he saw a tall girl standing by the rail. Her face was homely, gentle, and, above all, strong. He knew at once that she was from the Highlands, where such women have been bred since the beginning. Culloden had sent the McDonalds across the sea two centuries before, but at the sight of her his blood went coursing back to the old clans. She saw it, and gave him a straight look without curiosity or fear.

Within a year she had come back to marry him and put his neglected garden to rights. She learned to run levels, and used to ride down the line in the cab or tramp through the forest beside him, knitting without looking down. They were happy with the deep stoic happiness of the Scots, though at times she grew sad and lonely. She would go off by herself, and he could hear her in the distance singing the Skye boat song:

"Speed, bonny boat, like a bird on the wing,
  'Onward' the sailors cry,
Carry the lad that's born to be king
  Over the sea to Skye."

Her head would go up, and her low voice shiver with a defiant ring which took no reckoning of the poor ruined prince now crumbling in his grave as he had crumbled in his life generations before.

As the years passed, the pine woods were slowly drained of their turpentine. The trees were still mighty, but each dark trunk bore a long pale herringbone scar, stretching as high up as the pullers would reach, at its bottom a little rough-hewed slot into which the precious sap oozed down every spring. The supply was failing, and the demand as well, for the iron and steel ships they were building now had small use for naval stores.

McDonald from his window watched the dwindling stream of freight. He had long since stopped paying off his debts and had begun to borrow again. He saw his earnings of years and, at last, the very life of his road slowly flowing away. It was as if the great forest from which that life had come was silently taking it back to itself again. He used to gaze out over the soft level floor of tree-tops not with any fear or depression, but wondering deeply and sturdily what he should do. At last he saw in the papers the news that he had long been waiting for. He looked on the waving, whispering tops that night with a certain shame and awe, and next morning he started north to talk with hard-faced men.

In six months the lumbermen came in, jovial, drunken vandals who descended roaring from the train and skirmished with all who appeared on the streets that night. Here and there along the road they set up their ramshackle sawmills, crazy sheds from which came shrill, purposeless toots, wisps of steam and, endlessly repeated, a high-pitched groan as each cradled log struck the spinning saw. Slowly the heaps of ruddy, golden sawdust grew until they seemed like the burial mounds of the old giants who had there been sacrificed. The log wagons rutted their twisting roads back into the hills, through the great raw stumps and the heaps of dying slash, ever seeking the quavering cry of "Timber!" and the crackle of branches and groan of the heart pine which followed it. They came back, padding noiselessly over the bark and sawdust; only the complaining axles told of their mighty burden. The deer and the wildcat fled before them to the mountains of the west, and the little gray foxes crowded into the branches and lived precariously on the dark-furred swamp rabbits. Down by the sidings, heaps of rough-sawed lumber, a light, sharp yellow, shone in the raw light that now flooded for the first time those unaccustomed places. There were sturdy blockhouses of joist and scantling, and fan-shaped piles of sagging boards, while now and then a twelve-inch beam, destined for some distant, mighty task, basked its broad sides, still dripping from the saw.

The railroad flourished, and McDonald was happy again. The menace of the lean years had passed; he was once more paying off his debts; once more he had become a power in the land, a dispenser of prosperity to whom others turned deferential, hopeful faces; and above all he had now a child, a daughter, Flora. Small wonder he failed to see that his fortune was founded on nothing less and nothing more than the ruin of the countryside. Like the great pines that had fallen before him, he was in turn to stand, proud in the memory of countless frustrated storms, until disaster's unforeseen, keen edge should lay him low.

The first stroke came one evening in spring. He was sitting on the porch, his long square-tipped fingers were locked on his knee, and in the circle of his arms his little girl was curled up asleep like a puppy. Straggling pines barred the deep, rich sky; shadowy mockingbirds busied themselves after twilight insects; down in the yards he could hear the somnolent, metallic breathing of an engine.

His wife came to the door; even in the failing light he could see the startling pallor of her face. He would have sprung up, but she saw the child and stretched out a hand.

"No," she said,—her voice was taut and whispering,—"it's come to me. The doctor said it would."

He could almost see the yearning glow of her eyes as they strained to make out his figure and the child's. The next instant she had slipped inside the house. All down his back the primeval hackles rose at the unseen menace of the enemy. He sat numb, while three chill, tingling waves of dread swept quickly over him. Then he raised himself by his will and, swinging the child into a chair, passed with quiet swiftness through the door. He found her on a wide sofa near a small ivory-shaded lamp. She was curled up cunningly, in the same way as the child outside, a position incongruous and touching in one of her years. She was dead, but at the last a faint flush had come back to her face, an exquisite afterglow. He came no nearer, but dropped on his knees like a peasant before a wayside shrine.

Now the struggle against failure began—a struggle as bleak and endless as the moors which had bred the Mc-

Donald stock. Almost imperceptibly, timber became scarcer and poorer. Instead of the sinewy stringers of clear heart pine, in time only shingles, slats, and crate-boards came out, the off-scourings of the forest. And across the waste lands spread the useless scrub oaks in puny triumph over the old masters.

Along the coast the new ships of iron were bigger. Each year fewer of them could make the river port to the coast; slowly it withered away. The tall, serene houses of the old merchants and sailing masters passed shabbily into the hands of petty tradesmen. The tide of commerce receded, leaving at length only an impassive flotsam stranded in the town—Negroes, Portuguese, some Swedes, and Yankees. One by one the ships lanterns over the doors of inns and drinking places went out.

Of the railroad and its business nothing at length remained except a small traffic in grains and cheap manufactured goods that were carried by a single dingy engine over the crumbling line to the port and the scattered dead hamlets along the way. Nothing remained but that and old man McDonald himself. He used to sit on the porch every evening to see the only train come by. It would have been hard for a stranger to place him. More than anything else he might have been taken for a sheriff or a master engineer. His clothes were not those of a workman, but they could be worked in. His frame was heavy and blocklike. At rest he seemed made of concrete, but he moved with a swiftness and certainty that had about them almost slighter and taller than he really was. His face was ruddy with a grim, humourous kindness that disconcerted small minds. His eyes were like the muzzle of his gun, steel-gray, with an impersonal threat in their black depths. His gray hair grew thickly in wind-tossed eddies, and he carried his head thrust a little forward, with the face upraised, like a seaman fronting a storm.

Now as he sat there holding his great, heavy watch in his hand he heard the distant whistle of the locomotive and saw the creeping smoke-serpent draw nearer over the tops of the trees. It ended in a curling black cloud as the fireman threw on more pine knots. The next moment the grotesque front of the engine appeared round the bend. She was an antique wood-burner, with a funnel-shaped stack and a wide-spreading cowcatcher, like a prim old lady's crinoline. She passed with prodigious, woolly puffs and unearthly clankings, a string of box-cars clattering behind. Old man McDonald watched the Negro train hand shambling along the tops, setting the hand brakes for the hill. The train descended into the town, clanging the engine-bell.

He looked at his watch to note her time. He always did this, although for many years it had not even faintly approached the schedule. Still, he liked to know every day how much was the deviation.

The night closed in with the suddenness of a stage scene. His old engine, lighting up the belly of her own smoke, moved to her berth in the yards; lights winked here and there in the town, and the casual noises of a slipshod existence floated up to where he sat. The frogs began their harsh, unvarying iteration. Suddenly, coming swiftly from far away, he heard a stirring sound of smooth power, then saw a streaming blaze of lights as the Great Southern express rushed in. Her groaning brakes and shivering exhaust told of her might as she pulled up at the station. She lay there, purring with iron sternness. As the brakeman's lantern swung at the rear, she gave the first of the great, compact, measured coughs that were to send her on her way. With a spasm she spun her drivers in a shower of sparks, and then, cresting the grade, hummed down the line.

Old man McDonald sat with the sound still ringing in his ears, thinking of the flimsy rattle of his makeshift train. Inside he heard the gentle clink of china and turned his head slowly. His daughter, in the dining room, was putting the supper things away. Nothing had been changed in the house since that fatal night, nor ever would be, he thought grimly, as long as the two of them survived. They still ate their fare, now plain and meager, off mahogany and plate. He could see the old sideboard, whose lustrous, ruddy wood received deep into itself the reflection of the silver candlesticks. His mind wandered over the house, its sturdy furnishings of oak and pine, the foolish little odds and ends she had brought in and cherished with a childish care—earthenware vases, a wavy mirror with black-and-gilt frame, a rude print of Robert Bruce. He thought with a pang of the cedar closet upstairs where lay in even rows her beautiful dower linen. He took a sharp breath and threw up his head a little as he had a habit of doing at such times.

Through the window he could see Flora, a well-knit girl with a broad waist, but a quick, graceful carriage of the head. Her face was very forceful, and at the same time had an open doglike friendliness that covered the unknown depths below. She held a silver dish against her breast, polishing it round and round with a cloth. She was whistling in a soft, measured sort of whisper, a habit of her father's. He smiled as he watched her. She looked up and grinned affably out toward where he sat. "Coming out, Father," she said in the soft, but rugged, way of the Scotch Southerner.

Soon she appeared and sat on a chair beside him, and both looked out over the lights of the town for a while.

"Tired?" he said.

"Middling," she answered. "I oiled the big table today." They talked without looking at each other. He considered her remark for a moment, then said:

"The house looks mighty nice; everything—mighty nice."

This was spoken in a ruminating tone, as a soliloquy. By this device old man McDonald saved his own self-respect and spared her the intolerable mortification of having to receive a compliment. But it was perilous ground, and she quickly changed it.

"Are you going down the line tomorrow?"

"I reckon not. I was just looking at those two old engines in the yard. Expect I'll have to go over them. They are plumb rusty—both. Plumb rusty," he repeated after a long pause.

She moved slightly, but did not speak. Old man McDonald could not know that his words had suddenly flooded her with a strange, grotesque, yet passionate, longing to pick him up and rock him like a baby in her arms. She did, indeed, start impulsively to touch his worn sleeve in pity, but came to herself before she had done so. He sat, with no feeling of pity for himself, oblivious of his escape.

They talked no more. Here and there in the town the lights were going out. They rose and went to bed.

Early next day he started work. The yard, such as it was, lay in an unfrequented field that had been his father's. It was skirted by young pines, and along it, laid on the old furrows, ran two sidings. They were filled with the last crumbling relics of the old man's rolling stock: a string of boxcars with bulged and gaping sides; the blank, dust-filled windows of a coach; a miraculous caboose of local construction that looked a little like a stranded tug, a little like a suburban villa; and at the farther end the engines, so incrusted and immovable that they seemed to be two petrified antediluvians plunged through eternity in their vast bucolic reverie.

But despite their appearance they had been well cared for and could be easily put in running order. Old man McDonald began inspecting the first of them. His square figure heaved itself nimbly all over her, like a black bear in a grove of trees. Then he set to work.

First, he took the hooded cover off the stack and the housing off the cab and stowed them in a boxcar. Then with waste and a bucket of turpentine he cleaned the paraffin from the bright work, and touched up a few rusty places with emery paper. He filled the oil cups from a long-nosed can, and put oil-soaked waste in the packing boxes. After that he went tapping around with a copper hammer in search of loose bolts, tightening a nut now and then with his wrench. He was by nature a mechanic, and that part of the job gave him much pleasure. He whistled to himself with the same laborious whisper of his daughter.

He crawled underneath, and remained invisible for a long time, tinkering with the link motion and eccentric block. Only his musical breathings could be heard, as if the engine herself were already getting up steam. At last he emerged, solemnly content and heavily coated with grease and rust-flakes.

Matters now became serious, for he swung the arm of the near-by water-tank, and, coupling on an extra length of hose, began to fill the boiler. He mounted to the cab and peered intently into the firebox, listening to the water muttering around the tubes and watching for leaks. A few small rivulets trickled down the back, but he knew the heat would close them. From the woodpile he brought in pine-knots and hard wood and started his fire; then he delved into his pocket for corn bread and sat down on the fireman's seat to wait. From time to time he gazed out the window at the dense oily smoke mounting straight in the still air, or looked impatiently at the steam gauge, though he knew well that it would be an hour before it registered. He soothed himself by lighting his pipe with elaborate preparations and settled down to smoke. At length, quite unexpectedly, the indicator swung to 5. "Five pounds' pressure," he muttered, hurriedly knocking out his ashes. He opened the steam-cocks one after the other. The bottom two spluttered scalding water, but the highest cock hissed a sharp, clear jet of steam. He shut it off and waited intently, not excited, but quietly and deeply moved.

As she warmed up, the engine appeared miraculously to come to life. The stolid, dead surfaces began to glisten with the melting oil. In the cab, where the heat was greatest, the metal, so senseless an hour ago, seemed almost to pulsate and twinkle.

He fixed his eyes on the gauge. Slowly she climbed to 50. He opened the steam cocks again; only the bottom one showed water. More quickly the hand swung up to 100. He opened the cylinder drain cocks, and a splashing, feathered fountain of steam and water shot down along the rails. 120. He pulled back the throttle half an inch; the cylinders filled, and the forced draft whispered deeply in the smokebox. He waited no longer, but leaned out the cab window and opened the throttle. Slowly the drivers began to move; with the snort of a bison she turned them over; steam jets hissed beside the ponies; twice more, and she struck her stride, and carried the old man, grim and bright-eyed, out on the line.

From that time on he worked more and more on the road himself. It made him happy to be doing things with his hands again, and it reminded him of the old days, now more glowing and unbelievable than ever, when he had made the road out of nothing by the power of his strength and love. But in the evenings, when the unique, consuming single-heartedness with which he always labored had left him, he felt the slow pressure of fate and dreaded a future more incredible than the past—dreaded it all the more because he could not quite conceive it. He was being ruined; he could see that without shifting his seat, and Flora would go down with him to whatever obscure disinheritance awaited ruined men. That was where his hurrying thoughts paused. He had never before considered ruin long enough to picture what became of the men it overtook, still less their women. His imagination had gone other ways, always building, building.

As for seeing himself without the road, it was harder still. He would think about it tenaciously until at times he ceased to believe in his own existence. He was always glad when Flora came out to sit silently beside him and restore him to his world.

So he went on, working harder by day and more puzzled in mind at night. He saved at every possible point. He was not man of affairs enough to believe that if ruin was inevitable, it should, at least, by judicious financing, be converted from slow prostration into an abrupt, majestic cataclysm. He simply fought doggedly, directly, to keep things going.

He had no one working for him now except the fireman, a certain John Henry Moorehead. John Henry, as he was invariably called, was a limber youth of great seriousness, punctuated by outbursts of irresistible mirth. He came to his chief one day.

"Mr. McDonal'," he said respectfully, " 'spect I better quit."

"Why, John Henry, nothing wrong, is they?"

"No, sir; I've always been well used."

Old man McDonald was distressed. The departure of John Henry would be a welcome relief financially, but he was fond of the boy.

"Why, son, I'm sorry."

"I've got to go. But if you ever need me,"—he shyly stretched out a great hand,—"I'll come," he said, and turned away.

From this time on the old man ran the train himself, with his decrepit Negro gardener to fire for him. Little by little all the rest of his rolling stock was abandoned, and he settled down grimly to keeping the one train in order, and running it every day to hold his franchise. When he was younger he used to like to get the best there was out of an engine, and he knew how, too; but now he crept along, easing her down a mile before the stations and starting her by imperceptible degrees. He was hanging on to the last possible margin of safety. One morning as he waited beside the engine while she was being fired up the thought came to him that every bolt and plate in her stood between Flora, still a child, and some outer limbo beyond his horizon. When night came he would try again to picture it. He put a hand on the cylinder as if it were a talisman, and climbed into the cab.

That evening he sat straining into the dark, his hands curled over the arms of his chair like lion's paws, powerful, yet helpless. He was not afraid, but he hoped intensely to see for an instant what the future held, so that he might know how he should act. The darkness, blank at first, seemed after a while to weave with a motion that slowly took shape. At last he recognized it. It was the weaving of branches of great pines. Everywhere he looked the night seemed filled with those dark, tumultuous seas. The old pines, he thought, the old pines that were no more, come back to see his fall.

Suddenly he heard a brisk and hard-heeled step on the walk—the step of a Northern city-dweller. The next instant a dark little man had passed across the shaft of light and was wringing his hand.

"Mr. McDonald? Yes? This is Mr. Weiler. Well, Mr. McDonald, how are you now? Pretty good, yes? Good!"

He beamed affably, as though they were two old friends reunited after a trying separation, and made a sort of embracing gesture with his free arm. Then swiftly he drew up a chair to a confidential distance, and at the same time produced a cigar. Old man McDonald noticed that both waistcoat pockets were stocked with imposing rows of Havanas, like a duck-hunter's ammunition. He declined the cigar, and watched, mildly fascinated, as Mr. Weiler replaced it carefully and gave the pocket a dapper pat. It was absorbing to follow the pudgy agility of those hands, and he found himself a little disconcerted to hear Mr. Weiler remark in beaming tones:

"Certainly this is a fine location you got here, Mr. McDonald—and an elegant mansion and so forth."

"Well, sir, we're comfortable."

"Indeed, yes. I noticed it first thing I came into town. I was greatly imposed, and I said to the conductor, 'I bet that's where there lives a Southern gentleman.' Yes."

"What did he say?"

Little did the old man know how demoralizing was this simple question to Mr. Weiler's fictitious recital. But Mr. Weiler rallied.

"Oh, he said, 'Mr. Weiler,'—we had become fast friends, —'Mr. Weiler,' he says, 'let me tell you something. It certainly is.' "

This was said with an air of gentle solemnity which, after an impressive pause, swiftly passed into one of profound concern.

"I was waiting all the afternoon to see you, Mr. McDonald, because I heard that in the day you are engaged with your business affairs. So I did not come till now."

"Yes, sir, I was running the engine."

For a moment Mr. Weiler did not reply. When he did, it was with the sober weight of a businessman. Slowly he opened a discussion of general trade conditions in the North and spoke of bad times in a way that showed his responsibility for much that had been done to restore public confidence.

Old man McDonald listened closely, not always able to follow, but interested in this intimate view of a life so foreign—a life where men sat by telephones and made fortunes from the adventurous labors of other men, whose names they never knew, who were hired thousands of miles away to drill Persian wells, tap Congo rubber trees, or seine the Northwest salmon streams. These men at telephones built railroads that they never saw, bought them, and sold them among themselves like mule-traders on court day. He knew all this before, but now it first seemed real; more real, indeed, than Mr. Weiler himself, whom he could not help feeling a fabulous creature, an emissary from Bagdad. He reflected that, despite appearances, these men could perform some service; but at the same time it seemed much easier than in his world to make money without performing any.

"And now, Mr. McDonald, I would like to make you a proposition."

"Proposition." Mr. Weiler pronounced the word with a delicate, yet sonorous, impressiveness that was hypnotic, and clearly inspired and fortified Mr. Weiler himself. It was the only word in his vocabulary that retained much trace of foreign accent, though he used it most of all.

His proposition was to buy the road for a good price, all things considered; to buy it as old junk. Old man McDonald's head sank now, his hands curved stiffly. Mr. Weiler went on to outline glowingly the acts of Providence which had made such a uniquely liberal offer possible. He was representing an iron foundry that was short of ore on account of mine-strikes. They had decided to buy junk not from the dealers, whose practices he described, illustrated, and epitomized, but direct, through the medium of the frank, open, dependable Mr. Weiler. Old man McDonald listened motionless as Mr. Weiler warmed to his theme. In a sense Mr. Weiler was an artist; men very like him had come to America and become great violinists, etchers, sculptors. He loved business dealing as an art, irrationally, exultantly, for its own sake. He was carried away, and his voice flowed hypnotically on, melodious and full of passionate conviction not in the truth of his words, but in the artistry of his method.

The sale of the road, so inconceivable an hour before, became gradually a possibility, then finally loomed as the fortunate golden escape from the inexorable force of events. Mr. Weiler, quietly persuasive, yet intensely, electrically alive, was putting the finishing touches to his work.

Inside a door swung sharply.

"Who was that?"

"That was Flora, my girl."

The old man breathed, and heaved himself in his chair; he felt as though he were struggling back to dry land; then he moved his feet apart slowly one after the other.

"Well, sir, I'll think about it. Won't you come inside?"

But Mr. Weiler, watching, knew that the moment had passed, and after selecting an expression from his stock of farewells which he conceived to be dignified, yet intimate, left the house. He was to return the next night.

Old man McDonald heard the clicking, incisive footfalls

die away. At that distance Mr. Weiler seemed merely precise and active in a futile way. He was certainly inferior to the easygoing, but determined, men of the country; but up there on the porch he had shown a flash of peculiar power which they lacked. Was it simply the effect of his strangeness? The old man wondered in what that strangeness lay. He had traded with all sorts of men, Yankees, too, and always before he had read them well and relied on his judgment of them more than on written agreements. He wanted to understand Mr. Weiler before he did anything else, but he felt incapable of fitting him into the scheme of life as he knew it. If Mr. Weiler resembled anything, it was the little foreign man who years ago ran a pawnbroking and sailors' slops business down by the docks. But Mr. Weiler was far bolder and more elegant. He had, however, the same fat, quick hands and eyes at once sad and greedy.

At last old man McDonald turned from the problem and began to think of the business aspect of such a sale. Mr. Weiler had made it seem not only inevitable, but a peculiar triumph of sagacity and good fortune. All of that conviction did not depart with the tap of Mr. Weiler's heels. The old man knew it would be a good trade and leave him able to live decently, provided he were able to finance the road's debts along the involved, but apparently honorable, lines suggested by Mr. Weiler. Above all, there was no feasible alternative. He must anchor himself to that, to that and the picture of Flora, silent, brave, but touchingly helpless, watching him board up the front door and then quietly setting out with him for—nowhere. The thought bowed him forward into the darkness, but he returned to it again and again, and clung to it to steady himself against the tides of hope and memory that might now carry him to disaster as irresistibly as they had before carried him to success.

Flora came out. She moved Mr. Weiler's chair away a little and sat down.

"Who was that, Father?"

"I don't just know."

"A Yankee?"

"I couldn't tell. Maybe. I reckon so."

"I heard what he was saying."

"He wants to buy the road."

"I know—for junk. Do you reckon you'll sell?"

"It's a mighty good chance. I expect there won't be another."

Their talk ended—ended, as always, where most talk would have begun. They sat on, the old man engulfed in the struggle, and the girl frightened not at the event, but at herself, for she had made up her mind.

He must be getting old, he thought, so fast the fragmentary memories hurried through his mind. He lost the thread of reasoning, and surrendered to them at last. He had a glimpse of one of his old work gangs side by side along the rail, hunching their backs all together in short lifts, shifting the track; then he was sloshing along the wharf side against a norther, going to meet a Greenock tramp for which he had waited a year. He heard the click of the switch-points as his first engine, with him at the throttle, came off the Great Southern track to his own, and he felt the tug of the last car when the trestle crackled down. And through it all, now faint, now clear, came the murmur, mournful, strong, of pines in the deep-sea wind. He rose as if he were breasting it, and Flora followed him.

The next day passed in a dream of agony. His steady, well-knit mind was working like a beaver, buttressing itself against the poundings of his heart. By suppertime all was settled, but only once before in his life had he ever felt so tired. His daughter joined him afterward without clearing the table.

She looked at him. He turned his gaze to her childish face and saw the unbelievable woman in her eyes. Confused, he shifted it to the fading hills.

"I'm going to sell. It's the only thing."

"Father, don't!"

That shivering ring! He had never thought to hear it again. The old words sounded in his brain:

> Carry the lad that's born to be king
> Over the sea to Skye.

But he shook his head.

"We can't keep her running. What's going to become of you? I wouldn't if I could help it."

"I wouldn't whether I could help it or not. That man!"

He grinned.

"I expect he's honest."

But while he was laboring the point, her mind went back to her desire.

"Did you want money when you were younger?"

"Not much."

"Did mother?"

"No."

"You wanted to make the road run, and she wanted to help you."

"I reckon so."

"Well, that's what I want." She just touched him on the sleeve; then she started in. At the door she turned. "That man!" she said darkly, then disappeared. He could hear a short laugh trailing behind her.

Profound and painful adjustments were taking place in old man McDonald's mind. He had thought out his decision and taken it to protect his daughter, and now in some unfathomable manner she made him seem ever so slightly ludicrous and trivial. He might have been her small child whom she had detected being corrupted by a bad little boy. That was the way she had treated the business. But there had been nothing patronizing; he admitted that. And there had been something else that he would not forget.

She had grown up without his knowing it. He must have been asleep not to see it before. Suddenly the memory of John Henry flashed into his mind, and he recalled a hundred little circumstances to which he had been blind. John Henry had gone away to make some money before he asked her. Perhaps he had asked her. Well, he was a good boy.

Punctually, Mr. Weiler came. He performed the same ritual with the cigar, then started to talk. That afternoon old man McDonald had seen him looking over the road, but he was too familiar with it himself to realize that an inspection by a stranger would make its sale seem a foregone conclusion. Mr. Weiler had no doubts of the outcome, but he was irresistibly impelled to finish his speech of the night before. This he did.

"Ain't that so, Mr. McDonald?" he ended, with a perforating gesture of the index finger.

"I reckon so. But, Mr. Weiler, I don't believe I'll sell."

Mr. Weiler scarcely paused, but plunged again into the discussion in order to straighten matters out as he could easily do. But he did not get far.

"No, sir, I reckon I won't sell."

It was said in a shy and hesitating tone, but Mr. Weiler recognized, with a dreadful acuteness, that behind it lay centuries of a grim Northern breed. He was struck speechless in a way that he had never been before. He was frantic at being so abruptly balked without even the chance to show his cleverness. Yet in his despairing rage one idea persisted above all others. That was to make a stately final impression on old man McDonald.

After a heavy silence Mr. Weiler rose and stood rigid. "I am certainly astonished. I made this expensive trip thinking that of course you would be interested in my magnificent proposition. Good-by."

He bowed from the hips and vanished.

The next morning dawned in a sudden brilliant flash, and old man McDonald rose up in his bed and began to pound his chest mightily as he remembered the night before. Suddenly he felt his heart miss a beat, then two, and as he tried to get to his feet he seemed to slip and plunge into a pool of black oblivion. He sank back to the pillow, and raising one arm with an effort of will, he knocked on the wall.

Behind his steadfast, even gaze in the last two days there had raged a battle as intense, as merciless, as destructive in its sphere as any struggle which men commemorate by statuary and legal holidays. His body, square and hardy, but toilworn to the core, had given way.

For a week he lay there, and no train ran. No words could tell more than that of his suffering. The future was hopeless. He had missed his chance. Perhaps he could get Mr. Weiler back, but it would be a bitter defeat. He would write and tell him.

"Dear sir: I beg to advise you that, owing to my heart having unexpectedly got bad"—something like that. He reached for a financial newspaper to find the address of the firm. As he turned the pages a headline caught his eye. "Southern Harbor Development Co." New Orleans, probably. They were growing fast down there. A familiar name stared at him from the column of type. He began word by word to read the lines. His great hands gripped the paper till it trembled; then two tears twisted down his lined face. They were going to dredge the port at the end of the line. The old-time railroad days would come again. He pounded on the wall with both fists.

"Flora! Flora!"

Standing by the bed, she read the paper that he thrust silently into her hands.

"Take that down to the bank and ask them if they'll keep me going for a year."

"Father," she murmured, and shyly patted the worn, gay quilt.

"Honey," he said, "go on along," and turned his face to the wall.

She came back beaming, and panting like a terrier.

"They say they will if it's so."

He grinned dryly, then eyed her solemnly.

"They's a great future for this yer road," he announced, and leaned back, contented.

For a week he lay there like some strong, inoffensive animal driven to bay for causes he could not understand. Friends at the bank were to take charge of starting the road again, and the old man was filled with forebodings of their well-meaning incompetence.

One morning Flora was sitting in the room, going over his papers and letters, trying to help him all he would let her, for he had tired rapidly in the last few days. His face was still ruddy, his mouth the same straight line; but he could not hide the great weariness in his eyes. The papers rustled, her voice murmured as she read, and the old man, gazing into space, seemed drifting far away. Then faintly, below the house, climbing nearer, they caught the familiar, lugubrious clanking and flat, shallow puffings of the old wood-burner. She went to the window just as the little train lurched round the curve.

"Father, they've got her running again! She's all shined up. Two boxcars—and the caboose—and"— she scarcely breathed—"John Henry."

She gazed, rapt, at the train. Suddenly, she felt that he had moved. She looked around. He was standing beside her, incredibly old, his eyes blazing, the great gold watch trembling in his hand. He turned toward her with a touch of formal deference.

"By God! sir—" She never knew whether in that final moment he failed to recognize her, or whether at last he saw her for what she was. "By God! sir—on time!" And old man McDonald slipped quietly to the floor.

Elms and Fair Oaks

He always struck me as a futile old man, my grandfather. Nice and kindly and all that sort of thing, but somehow he just didn't seem to have the stuff. I don't know how to put it, but I'd been to one of the big schools where they teach the fellows to make good, and I could see that there was something missing in him. When I was a little kid at home I thought he was fine, but after I'd been at school long enough to learn some of the things that count I found out that the old man didn't have them. Everybody liked him, but that was all. They called him "Gramper"; everybody. Still when I was ready to leave for college it seemed like only the decent thing to go and say good-by. Especially as he'd gone to Princeton himself, some time before the Civil War. And anyway I'd noticed that the really big men at school were always nice to an older man, even when you could see they knew he hadn't the stuff.

He was sitting in his living room before the fire. The place had been the same for years; lots of books, an old globe of the world, and a picture of Lincoln. He turned slowly as I came in. He looked like an old lion. That was the funny thing about him; you would think if you saw him that he was a great man.

"Well, Gramper," I said, "I'm going off to college tomorrow. Thought I'd come and say good-by."

The old man raised his big, gray head and then looked into the fire.

"Going off to college, eh? Going to Princeton." He stroked his neat, short beard.

"Princeton," he muttered. "It's a queer sort of a place unless it's changed, and I don't suppose it has, really. It gets hold of a man in a way none of the others do—gets hold of him whether for good or bad. Princeton made a lot of difference to me. I suppose you're busy getting ready?"

"No," I said. "I'll sit here for a little while."

Gramper nodded slowly toward a chair and looked at the bowl of his pipe.

"I went down to Princeton in the fall of '58," he said, "With a hair trunk and a new beaver hat. I suppose you knew?"

"I knew it was just before the war," I said. "But I didn't know about the hat."

Gramper smiled. "The hat," he said, "was the main thing. At least I thought so then. My father gave it to me the day before I left. It came from Philadelphia."

"I know," I said, "all hats come from Philadelphia."

"No, you don't know. Not at all. All the hats come from Philadelphia now, but then every town had its own hatter. No one my age ever had a hat from Philadelphia before."

"I expect you were pretty well stuck on yourself, Gramper," I said.

"Well, I might have been," he answered, nodding, "if I hadn't been so scared. You see it was a big thing in those days—to go away to college. A kind of scaring adventure. I was the only one from the academy here."

"I suppose it was quite a journey," I said. "Did you go by stagecoach or did they have the canalboats then?"

"Oh, I'm not quite as old as all that; the railroad was running; only, the engines were wood-burners. It went to Philadelphia and from there to New York along the canal. I remember I kept looking out after we left Philadelphia to see if I could make out the college buildings. But I could only see flat fields and sloping woods. Suddenly the conductor roared out 'Princeton!' in my ear. His voice lifted me right to my feet. I was very red and thought everyone in the car knew he meant me.

"The next minute I was standing in a ring of hack-drivers, a small ring, but very noisy. I picked out an old darkey in the background who looked comparatively respectable in a bleary way.

"On the way up the long hill I found out that the driver's reserve, which I'd thought came from delicacy of feeling, was really due to intoxication. But the horse seemed to know the way and we got along slowly.

"My room was in East College and the driver carried up my trunk. I gave him a quarter and he took off his hat and scraped a foot behind him.

" 'Ah thanks you, misto, Ah profoun'ly does,' he said, and then he looked to make sure no one was around.

" 'An don' fo'get Eustace,' he said, 'Frien' all young gempmum.'

"He rolled his eyes like a stage conspirator. 'Any li'l thing,' he said, 'any li'l thing,' and tiptoed out. Of course, I didn't know what he meant.

"That night I sat in my little room looking at my hair trunk. It was hard to believe that very trunk had stood the day before in my own room at home. It seemed as though I had gone such a long way since then.

"I could hear some one moving in the next room. It was another freshman, the janitor had told me. He began to sing a song about 'Eliza Jane.' I remember how funny it seemed the way he pronounced the words. I'd never heard a Southern accent before. But he could sing like anything, with a little kind of shuffle in the time that made my feet tap on the floor. There were a lot of verses and I began feeling better all the time.

"At last he stopped. That singing had given me a kind of bold, adventurous feeling. I wasn't that way by nature. But before I knew it I was pounding on the wall and calling out to him: 'Go on—sing some more.'

"That doesn't sound particularly bold, I suppose, but it really was for me.

"He hollered right back as if it was the most natural thing.

" 'Yankee!' he hollered, 'come on in here and I'll show you how to sing—and dance.'

"Well, then I felt a little awkward for having so much brass, but I got up and went into the room.

"There stood a tall, slim young man, with reddish hair." Gramper mused.

"Tall and slim," he went on, "with a lean, reckless face. He was standing, elegantly dressed, in a pile of belongings that he'd thrown everywhere. He bowed and held out his hand with a sort of mixture of formality and impudence.

" 'La Rue is my name, seh,' he said; 'from New Orleans!'

"I gave him mine and he asked me to sit down. We talked for a while. He was very much at ease and I was bashful and lumbering, I suppose. I told him I had enjoyed his song. When I said that he began to sing again:

'Li'l David, play on yo' harp—
Hallelu! Hallelu!
Li'l David, play on yo' harp—
Hallelu!'

"Then he whistled it, doing funny little gliding steps right there in the pile of clothes." Gramper hummed a bar, moving his square hands in rhythm on the arms of his chair.

"There wasn't much to it, but it made me tingle all over. It was so new and strange.

"Well, sir, that was the man, Larry La Rue. French and Irish—and imp of Satan.

"We stuck to each other from that time on. He was just the kind of fellow I wanted to be and couldn't. At first he kept me from getting too homesick. I asked him if he ever felt homesick himself.

" 'Well, if I do,' he said, 'd'yeh reckon I'm going to let on to these Yankees? No seh, I've got my tail over the dashboard and I'm bound to keep it there.'

"Later on things changed and I used to help him sometimes. I got him home once when he was pretty full—he'd started to shoot out the light on the president's porch with a horse pistol—and several other times.

"He was always like that. Right to the end whenever I saw Prexy Maclean sprinting across the campus in his galoshes and cloak, I knew that Larry was probably a few yards in front of him—but gaining.

"After the first year we had a room together. He called me Achates and let me get him out of scrapes with a sort of good-humored tolerance. One day, though, when another fellow tried to call me that, he turned on him like a flash.

" 'What do you mean, seh?' he said, 'by insulting my friend?'

"It was ridiculous, of course, but he had a small, cold voice when he was angry, and the fellow got red and apologized.

"He was just like a child," said Gramper gravely, "just like a child—he was wonderful.

"They were great days. In the spring we played town-ball and rounders. But the winter was the time for Larry. It was a cold, dull term, and he became one of a crowd who were bent on bringing conviviality into life by fair means or foul. They were mostly Southerners and belonged to a secret society that had been forbidden by the faculty like all the others.

"I first noticed that Eustace was hanging 'round a good deal. Larry used to call him a 'free nigger' in a way that made it sound as if that were as low as a human being could sink. And Eustace worshipped him. Larry made him confess that Eustace wasn't his real name—he'd just heard it in a play. His real name was Henry, but Larry said that was too high-toned and christened him 'Gomorrah' instead.

"Well, Eustace was always shuffling back and forth with messages, and in the end Larry told me what it was all about. He and his friends were to have a dinner the next night at the tavern in town. That was against the rules of course, but when the time came they slipped out. The tavern was just across Nassau Street, so it was easy. But about ten o'clock I could hear the noise of their cheering in my room. I knew that couldn't last long, so I went out to see how things stood. I sneaked along by the church and across the street. There, sure enough, was a tutor coming toward the inn. I just had time to duck into the coach-yard and up the back way to where they were. I could hear Larry's voice as I came up the stair. He was saying, 'Gentlemen, I give you the sacred rights of each sovereign state and each sovereign individual.' They started to look at me very coldly as I burst in. But I just said, 'Old Noggs—out front,' and the sovereign individuals were out the back door, climbing fences in all directions, and me with them helping Larry, who would start to climb every fence six feet before he got to it.

"None of them was caught, but there was no chance of another party at the tavern after that.

"You know," said Gramper with an uncertain smile, "I've always regretted that I didn't have the sense to say, 'Gentlemen, I give you Old Noggs—on the front pavement.' That would have been good. It's just the sort of thing Larry would have done.

"What was I telling about? Oh, the next thing was a party in one of their rooms. It really didn't amount to much, but they had got Eustace to smuggle in quite a lot of port, and this time the tutors caught them all.

"Prexy Maclean let them know that it would go a good deal easier with them if they told him who smuggled the port. There was always something of the sort going on, and he wanted to stop it.

"They came back to our room to talk it over. Some were

in favor of telling, on the grounds that it would save their skins and at the same time rid the college of a pernicious influence. But Larry was indignant. 'I resent that suggestion!' he said, 'most vehemently. I consider it beneath our dignity to save ourselves at the expense of a free nigger.' So they didn't tell and were rusticated for four months.

"The fall of junior year was '60 and we began to hear of trouble between the North and the South. It worried us all a little, because nearly half the men were Southerners, of course, and our friendships were all mixed up together. The place was so beautiful—the old buildings and elms and green country—a great place to make friends. We were worried, though, when we read the papers and heard from home, but we never thought war would really come. We thought every one was like us. But toward spring some of the Southern men began to leave, and then all of a sudden one morning in April '61 we got the news that Sumter had been fired on. It was incredible. It still is—the most incredible day of my life. In other places they were full of excitement and patriotism—getting ready to fight. But in Princeton there was nothing but a kind of dumb sadness.

"That night Larry and I walked away off together. The elms were dark and soft in the starlight. The road was soft and dusty. We didn't say anything. Far away we heard the bell strike nine.

"I stopped and whispered, 'Larry, I hope it won't come. I hope it won't.'

" 'Won't come!' he said. "Don't be a fool. It has come.'

" 'I'm not,' I said, 'but you know.'

" 'I know,' he said, 'I'm the fool and always have been.

But I'd have been a heap bigger one if it hadn't been for you, Achates. I know that, too. I expect you thought I didn't. But you just always remember—' and before I knew it he put his arms around me and began to cry.

"I was trying to think of something to say to him when he looked up in his old way and started to sing:

'You might as well live in union,
You got to die.'

"We went back to our room.

"Early next week the Southerners all left together. Prexy Maclean made them a great speech and loaned them money to get home on.

"When it was time for them to go, the rest of us marched down with them to the railroad station. We carried their satchels for them.

"I was carrying Larry's, but, the first thing I knew, old Eustace had appeared from nowhere, the way he always did, and was taking it out of my hand. ' 'Scuse me, misto,' he said, 'but dis yer's ma bin'nes,' and he fell in at Larry's heels and never took his eyes off him. It was a busy day for the hacks, but he let some one else drive his.

"We straggled along in little groups; some of them were making a good deal of noise, some were very quiet. A few of the Southern men had Negro body servants, slaves they had brought to college with them. We knew these old darkies, of course, and had lots of fun with them, blaming all the trouble on them and getting them mixed up and indignant.

"But when the train came in the fooling stopped. We

shook hands awkwardly as if we were ashamed of what was separating us. Larry turned to Eustace and handed him a dollar bill, one of Prexy Maclean's. But the old negro drew back.

" ' 'Scuse me, no suh," he said, ' 'scuse me, no. You is de highes' gempmum das been to dis yer college since Ah come; de highes' gempmum. Ah des tote de bag down fo' de honor, dassall.' His voice broke and he bundled the satchel up the steps of the car.

"We just stood there watching the others get on board. As the train began to move, we gave three straggling cheers. They waved from the car windows.

"We were turning away when we heard a long high yell. There was Larry on the rear platform. His hat was off and he was laughing. I can hear him now. He was shouting,

" 'Good-by—you damn Yankees!'

"Well, after that college was just a sort of pretense. Men kept leaving to join the Union Army, and the next year, when people saw what the war really meant, most of the fellows who were of age went. We were seniors then. I'd hung back on one excuse or another, but, in my heart, it was because I didn't want to fight against Larry. In the end, though, I had to go. I joined the 300th Pennsylvania from home.

"I'd had military drill at the academy and they were short of officers then, so in four or five months I got my commission. I wasn't properly qualified, of course, but things were in a bad mess in those days and if I didn't take it, it would go to some political hanger-on. We were swamped with bad officers then. There was no system. As the war went on we got rid of them. Some were shot by firing squads, some by their own men, and a few by the Confederates—by mistake. That's a part of war you don't hear much about. Others were given small jobs where they could do no harm."

Gramper slowly knocked out his pipe.

"I was one," he said.

"At first, though, I got on well enough, and by '62 I was a captain—captain of Company E.

"We were fighting in the Peninsula, though there wasn't much fighting to it. We were always changing position and digging fortifications with nothing much to show for it so far as we could see. But our brigade was well officered and well disciplined by that time, and we didn't lose heart as much as some of the others. When we got to Fair Oaks, they put us in the centre of the line and told us we were going to be attacked. The men made bitter jokes about the honor, but they were proud, in a way, and we knew they would stay there. I was proud, too, until I heard that one of the regiments against us was the Louisiana Tigers.

"When morning came we were behind a stone wall and the enemy were in the woods on the opposite slope of the little swampy valley. My orders were to hold our fire till they struck the soft ground in the bottom and then to give a volley and fire at will.

"The day was still and bright and though we couldn't see them, we could hear their officers forming them up to charge.

"My men were biting their cartridge caps and spitting. I remember one new recruit about your age, near me, who tried to spit like the older men. But he couldn't. His face was gray and he couldn't spit at all.

"Then from the woods there came that wild shivery cheer. We knew it well by then, but we never liked it.

"There was a crackling of branches and the tattered, muddy lines broke out of the woods on the run. They were a tough-looking crowd. We could see the white of their check bones against their scrubby beards.

"We were well equipped and turned out like regulars, but I wished we looked rougher than we did when I saw them coming.

"Then as they hit the swamp, I saw an officer in the front rank take off his hat and jump ahead. It was Larry."

Gramper breathed hard.

"I couldn't give the order to fire.

"Our troops had opened on both sides of me and as the Confederates floundered through, I could see my lieutenants—looking at me. The men had sighted their rifles, but they were trained soldiers and there wasn't a shot.

"I kept staring at Larry. My God, would he never get out of the way?

"As they came out of the swamp, some of his own men passed him. He was covered for an instant and I gave the order. But it was too late—the next minute they were through the smoke of our volley, clubbing at our heads. We fell back.

"As we went down the hill I saw Larry standing on the stone wall. He was making a little bow and yelling:

" 'Good-by—you damn Yankees!' "

Gramper stared for a long while into the fire.

At last I asked, "Did you never see him again, Gramper?"

He raised his big head with a start and gave a short laugh.

"Larry? Oh no. I was sent to the rear in charge of army stores. After the war I looked for him. He was missing—missing since the battle of Fair Oaks."

He burnished the bowl of his pipe in the palm of his hand and cleared his throat. Then he looked at me with a smile.

"Those were great days," he said in a strong, clear voice, "at Princeton."

Bloodhound

THE crowd of black felt hats moved from the track.

"Hyer she comes. Hark to her whistle."

"That's good. They tell me with a bloodhound every minute counts."

"That nigger's had four hours' start right now."

"Reckon it was a nigger."

"It's a nigger. All this stealing around town's nigger work. And what white man would take a purple suit with yellow stripes?"

"All I hope, this dog can smell him. They tell me it costs the town fifty dollars to bring it here."

"Heyo, Will, you got a bloodhound aboard?"

"Sure have. Hyer's the man with him."

"Gentlemen, how you all?"

"Howdy."

"Now, gentlemen, stand back and give this dog room. Too many folks is liable to mess him up."

"Look at them great ears. A man could tie them under his chin."

"Now, gentlemen, whereabouts do we start?"

"Right yonder. See that sign 'Bullteel's Clothing Store'? Nigger taken the suit right off the hanger."

"That dog knows what he come for. Don't he walk proud, though?"

"He's a severe dog."

"They tell me, though, a bloodhound's gentle."

"Well, doggone if I'd love to hear one belling on my track."

"They say, though, he don't do nothing but smell and holler."

"That's all right, but, as the fellow says, does the dog say it? Yes, sir, I want to hear it from the dog, else I'm gone right now, I—"

"Now, gentlemen, stand back. Don't mess up the sidewalk. You Mr. Bullteel?"

"Yes, sir. Bring in your dog."

"Never mind that. Bring out the hanger the suit was on."

"You reckon he keeps the harness on that dog all the time?"

"I expect so."

"Sure he keeps it on. How could he stay with him else?"

"Yes, sir, without that harness that dog would fly."

"Watch him snuff that hanger."

"Hark to him snuff."

"Now, gentlemen, stand back."

"He's working the ground now. Now he's whimpering."

"Man, he's off."

"Come on, boys."

"Now, gentlemen, keep back."

"Doggone, he's bound to catch that nigger. He's straining in the collar."

"Oh, man, hark to him. I'd love mighty well to hear that tongue on a fox."

"Now he's hushed."

"Hold on, boys, don't push him. This cross street has him bothered."

"Stand still. Let's see what he will do."

"There he goes. Round the corner and down the hill. Right for Jim Crowtown."

"Didn't I say it was a nigger?"

"Bill, you and some others cut around ahead. Don't let any nigger leave on the other side. You all got guns?"

"We all got guns."

"Now, gentlemen, stay back. All these nigger tracks keeps him studying."

"Look at all the niggers disappear."

"Nothing but dust and doors a-slamming."

"Niggers sure despise a bloodhound."

"They say, though, a bloodhound's gentle."

"That's all right, but does the bloodhound say it? Yes, sir, I want to hear it from the bloodhound."

"Hush, he's hit off his loss. Come on."

"Now, gentlemen, keep back."

"If he branches off yonder they ain't but one house it can be."

"Well, there he goes. It's Sis Highpocket's."

"He's straining on it now."

"It's Sis Highpocket's. Look at him jump at that door."

"Stand back, gentlemen. Nigger, open that door."

"Come out, Sis."

"Sis, open that door."

"Take a run at it, Lon. Pull out your guns, boys, and go right in behind him."

"Hold on, gentlemen, till I get my dog away."

"All right, let's go. Everybody in."

"Oh, my sweet God, gentlemens, oh, my—"

"Hush your fuss, Sis. Who you got with you?"

"God is my judge and witness, gentlemens. They ain't been a man in this house since my man went on the roads."

"What you got on under that green wrapper, Sis?"

"Gentlemens, let me tell you the truth. I was just changing my closes to step over to town for my Saturday rations. I was—"

"What man you got here, Sis?"

"Gentlemens, I—"

"Look under the bed, Jeff."

"Oh, my sweet God, gentlemens."

"Yonder he is. I can see his feet. Come out, nigger. Grab his leg."

"Who's got the handcuffs? Nigger, hold out your hands. Anybody know this nigger?"

"Looks like one of them south Georgia niggers that's come in."

"That's what he is. It's them south Georgia niggers been raising all the fuss around here."

"Sis, what ails you? This is as sorry a nigger as ever I saw."

"He's yellow and he's puny."

"Can't you do no better than that, Sis?"

"Gentlemens, God is my judge and witness. I never seen this person before. He must have crope under my bed when I was sleeping. Black boy, don't you grin at me. I'll slap your head in, ape. Gentlemens, let me tell you the truth. This is a mighty big surprise. I declare—"

"Anybody find the suit? Cut open the mattress."

"Done cut it open. Pillows as well."

"Let's get out. Between nigger and feathers I'm about to lose my breath."

"Never mind the suit. We got the nigger."

"So long, Sis."

"Sis, you better tread light. When your Lundy gets off the roads he'll cut your liver."

"Gentlemens, ain't I told you—"

"We ought to tie a rope on this nigger."

"You know what we ought to do? We ought to tie this nigger up and whip him good."

"Road gang don't mean nothing to him. He'll get fat on the roads."

"Nigger, you want to be whipped?"

"No, suh."

"Heyo, here comes Hugh Dave. His face is afire and he's stepping high."

"Look at him raise his knees. That scoundrel sure loves his liquor."

"Howdy, Hugh Dave."

"Hi, boys, howdy. How you all come on? What's the fuss?"

"Nigger yonder been stealing."

"Nigger, you been stealing? Doggone my hide, you ought to be whipped. If they's anything I despise it's a stealing nigger. For two cents I'd lay onto you with a bull whip till you had the gospel in your soul. You hear me? Who caught him?"

"Bloodhound from Twelve Oaks."

"Bloodhound, come here. Raise up, dog. You and me

will finish this bottle together. Raise up, dog. Only don't mess up my clothes. They're new."

"Man, keep your liquor away from my dog."

"Whereabouts did you get that suit, Hugh Dave?"

"Taken it out of Bullteel's store. He was gone and I aimed to go on that Birmingham excursion, only I needed a suit and I was drunk."

"You're drunk now, Hugh Dave."

"Then I went to sleep and missed the excursion. And now look at my fix. I've the suit to pay for and I've slept in it already and my liquor is give out and it's a sorry blue-gum nigger suit, anyways."

"Doggone if that ain't the suit."

"Sure enough, that's the suit."

"Well, boys, it looks like this is the suit. Nigger, you listen. You can go this time, but mind how you carry on around here."

"Yes, Suh."

"Man, what ails your bloodhound that we paid fifty dollars for?"

"You lay off this dog. He's caught twenty-nine niggers and a white man in the last three years. And two of them was hung."

"Looks like they hung the wrong niggers if this fyce dog caught them."

"You call my dog a fyce, you—"

"Now, gentlemen, gentlemen—"

"Well, then, let him lay off my dog."

"Friend, they is no complaint about your dog. Ain't that a fact, boys?"

"Sure is. A dog can't always be right."

"And it's a mighty good thing for this community—to bring in a bloodhound."

"Yes, sir. It will keep the Negroes quiet for some little time."

"Why, man, this bloodhound has done a thousand dollars' worth of good."

"What this town needs is a bloodhound."

"Well, gentlemen, times are hard with me. For three hundred dollars—"

"Well, boys, I reckon we better be getting back to town."

Away! Away!

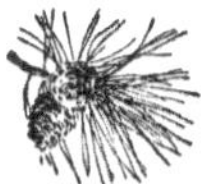

UNDER the bare oaks in front of the kennels the man stopped his Model-T Ford. It stood shivering until he shut the motor off. As he climbed out, the top trembled and swung. He knocked his hands together and looked at the oaks, black against the whitewashed kennel fence, and at the silvery roof of the barn beyond. A hound spoke; he stopped knocking his hands and tucked them in the front of his jeans. Then he turned toward the stone house. His face was clay below his black slouch hat, and under his thin moustache you could tell his teeth were rotten. He saw MacSherrill on the porch and started up the path between the dead rose bushes.

"Howdy," he said. "You want to buy a fox?"

"No," MacSherrill said.

The man turned round and started back to the car. Below his sleeveless leather jacket his jeans were worn whitish on the seat. They were too short and they hiked up and down.

He knocked his hands together and turned the engine over; it missed. MacSherrill dropped his morning paper on the porch.

"Hold on," he said.

The man came back up the path and stood looking at MacSherrill over the porch rail.

MacSherrill leaned forward. His pigskin gaiters creaked on his shoe tops, he did not look at the man, he looked down at his gaiters.

"Where did you get him?" he said in a low voice.

The man jerked his head like a bird.

"Mountains yonder. Dove Cove."

"How old is he?"

"It's a sow. She's growed."

"Is she sound?"

"Garnteed. One toenail off, that's all."

MacSherrill kept looking at his gaiters. The man, he knew, was looking at him. But with no meaning; as if they were both cows.

"How much?"

"Well, friend, times is hard—"

MacSherrill reached in his pocket. He laid a five dollar bill on the porch rail. The man folded it in a wad.

"Where you want her?"

"Not here." MacSherrill obliged himself to look at the man; his teeth were rotten sure enough. "Go on down towards Little Rodney and across the graded road. In a mile you'll come to a red barn and a Negro tenant-house with a hound pup chained in the yard. Ezra Taylor is the Negro's name. It's on his mail box. Leave the crate there."

The man went back to the Ford. This time it started. MacSherrill picked up the paper. The fox was off the place. If that car had started the first time he wouldn't have bought her. He stuck his hands in the pockets of his old cord breeches. It mighty near did start, too.

He heard the kennel gate bang. Milton, the head Negro, was coming to the house. He had strings tied around his trousers below the knees and a Fair Isle sweater that MacSherrill had given him eight years ago, with blue flannel patches on the elbows. He was light moving, bandy-legged and severe. Behind him the old lame hound, Tawney, limped with dignity; he looked up at MacSherrill and made a solemn movement with his white-tipped tail. At the place where the mountain man had reached the path he stopped; his grave gray-muzzled face dropped down, hung over the frosted stones with wrinkled studious brows.

About the third dead rose bush from the house Milton took off his peaked cap; but with no deference. He had a quick mean little head like a snake's.

"Everything all right?" MacSherrill said.

"Yes, sir."

"Raffle sound?"

"Tried him on the long rope. He trotted out pretty glib."

"Better keep cold-water bandages on just the same."

"You aim to ride him Saturday?"

"Yes. Lots of folks. Yankees down from New York; for Lincoln's birthday. It's a holiday there."

"That's a good lookin' horse if he don't kill hisself."

"He's all right. He's got sense."

"Got sense. Just don't give a damn."

"Well what about the hounds?"

"All right. Joker been fighting again last night. I whipped him about it."

"That's right."

"Yes, sir. Can't have no more hounds cut up with his doin's. Scarce of hounds right now."

"That's a fact."

MacSherrill looked down toward the road. Old Tawney, having trailed the mountain man to where the car had stopped, quartered the ground with slow methodical steps. He met the raw scent of gasoline and sneezed, flapping his ears under his chin. He recovered himself and stood reflecting. Then he reached up into the air and swung his muzzle in a trance-like quest. He opened his mouth and sounded his deep echoing note. An answer burst out behind the kennel fence, a clamor of squeals and roars and babbles that was cut off, sharp as a knife stroke, by Milton's shout.

"You hounds!" he said. "That drive them crazy. Ain't heard Tawney speak since he quit hunting." He turned to MacSherrill. "Somebody been by here? Heard a car."

"A mountain fellow."

"He had a fox in that car," Milton said. He looked at MacSherrill. "You buy him?"

"No," MacSherrill said. "Is there anything else?"

"That feed bill man come by last evening."

"What did he say?"

"Said he was going to wait till you come."

"What did you say?"

"Said you was gone to Washington for a few days."

"Anything else?"

"No, sir. Reckon I better go over to Little Rodney for feed and such for a while."

"What's the matter with Burge's in town?"

"It's all right, I reckon."

"Have any trouble there?"

"No, sir. Couldn't say trouble."

"All right. Better go to Little Rodney."

Milton went back down the walk. He did not put his peaked cap on till he got to the third rose bush again. But there was nothing respectful about it. "I sure would fire that Negro," MacSherrill thought, "if I could find another like him." But to turn him off he'd have to pay him the wages he owed; have to pay him the money he had borrowed from him, anyway. He took a sheepskin coat from a nail on the white-painted stone wall. He might as well go over and see about things.

The Buick's nose, with a lap robe over it, was looking out of a shed behind the house. He threw the lap robe in the back. The seat was cold but the engine started right away. Old Tawney, standing by the kitchen, looked at him intently as he went by. "God damn," he said in a low voice. "Why can't you keep your mouth shut?" He drove around the far end of his house and back along the country road. Behind the plank fence, the cedars in front of his white stone house looked black in the cold bright sun, the oaks in front of the kennels looked black, too, and the clay of the road and where the dead winter grass had been worn away was brick red. Down the gentle grade he could see a scope of country; melted frost made the fields of stubble wet and shiny; the top rails of the fence shone, too; the fields of winter wheat were dark maroon.

It was a fine bold piece of country: no wire, all good fences and mostly grass clear to the mountains. Used to have some big runs over this country when his father had the hounds. But now there were no foxes. He couldn't afford to hunt it right and so the farmers had taken to shooting them. Foxes had moved out to the mountains.

Beyond the nearest dark-red ridge another shoulder, long and gray green, rose up as he rolled along. And far beyond it, where the checkered flecks of color and the lavender hedgerows blended together, the mountains stood up sharp and dark.

It could be a good country still. A better country than in his father's day. More open, cleaner. And the foxes would come back, if they were given a chance—all this trapping, shooting; poison even. He struck a cold fist on the wheel.

If things would never change; that's what he'd ask. His father had hunted the country, shown great sport, lived off his land like a gentleman; grandfather too; and probably a lot more before that. The house was old and they'd always had it. Always kept hounds there too. But now, what with damage claims and shooting foxes—And a man now couldn't even live off the land, let alone keep a pack of hounds. No, it was all changed and spoiled. Why? He knew how to farm and how to hunt a pack of hounds. He had been raised to it and it was in his blood. And it was all he did know or want to know. Why shouldn't he be able to do it? Dodging feed bill men.

Not only feed bill men. He still hadn't caught up on his Buick payments. And Raffle; he'd have to do something about him or Rooney would come and take him away. He'd used up all the merchants in the country; he'd used up all his kinpeople, even Cousin Sue. One of these days somebody would start a move against him. Then they'd all come down and everything would go: the long narrow stone house, the barns, the fields, the spring house and the winter pasture, the hounds. The Jones brothers with their high hats and four-piece band, out on the front lawn, auctioning it all off piece by piece. He'd be let save out something on his homestead exemption; he'd pick out some farm tools and his grandfather's horse pistol and two good bitches—Tansy, probably, and Myrtle. Who would buy the place? Some town merchant; or a Yankee; or would the bank just take it over? God damn such a way of living. If he'd known what it all was coming to he'd have gone to West Point instead of being fired from the University. Might have been a Major by now.

Far in to the right, against a dark high wood, the four columns of the old Kincaid place looked white and pure. A Northern man had rented it. Named Tatum. He was thinking of buying it. That was different though; all the Kincaids were dead. The best thing that could happen would be to have that Tatum buy it. He was all right; didn't know a thing in the round world about hunting and never would, but crazy over it and willing to put out the money. Big money. Only it had been a sorry season. Days sitting outside the woods in the cold or rain and Tatum there on one of his three thousand dollar hunters not knowing or caring about what the trouble was, just wanting a chance to ride at all those fences stretching down the valley. Meanwhile, of course, those real estate buzzards from round Shelby had got hold of him, told him what runs the Shelby County were having every day. And now Tatum wanted to have this Lincoln's birthday meet right on his place. And draw the swamp and the wood around it so all his Northern visitors that didn't ride could have a chance to see it. Sweet God Almighty; there hadn't been a fox on the Kincaid place since the old Judge died.

With a couple of big bounces he crossed the state highway and went on between stark elms to Ezra Taylor's. The red barn was patched with weathered boards and pieces of tin. The cabin of squared logs was whitewashed and so was the picket fence. You could see it was a pretty good sort of Negro's. He stopped and blew the horn. In the yard a blue-ticked hound pup, half grown, gave a sweet ringing bark and then curvetted and bowed himself down. He had been obliged to bark but it had been against his own better judgment.

Ezra came out of the mouth of the red barn. He had been a preacher once and always wore a long black coat and a collar with no tie and a pair of gold spectacles that he bought at the auction of Colonel Rawley's place. His mustard-colored trousers were tucked into a pair of canvas leggings.

"Ezra," MacSherrill said, "did a man come by here?"

Ezra came up to the car. He raised his woolen cap with earmuffs tied together on top. He set it back very straight on his gray head.

"Yes, sir," his voice was deep, and heavy with good judgment. "She's in the barn." He put a dark gray hand on the door handle. "Yes, sir," he looked away off with great concentration. "She's in the barn."

"Whereabouts?"

"In the calf stall."

"Well, you put her up in the back of the loft. Right now."

Ezra's manner faded. "In the loft, Mr. Rad?"

MacSherrill tapped the wheel with his finger. "If anybody asks you, you don't know anything about this. Not a thing. Now listen. You know that rich Northern gentleman that's rented the Kincaid place, Mr. Tatum?"

"Yes, sir. Talk like maybe he's going to buy that place and settle. Some say yes and some say no."

"Never mind. On Saturday we're going to meet right on that place. Now listen. I'm going to try the woods in front of the house first and then the swampy bottom; there's nothing there and ain't been for years. When that's over I come back up the hill and put into the big woods above the house. That will all take twenty minutes. That gives you time, while the folks are following me, to ride in on the back side with this fox in a bag. You can see the mountains from there. Head her right for them and give her a light switch as she leaves the bag."

The Negro looked important; he ran his gray hand up and down the door-frame slowly as if he were polishing it.

"Now," MacSherrill said, "now." He reached across the seat and gently thumped the Negro's hand with his fist. "You come out on the Taylor Town road and don't let anybody see you come out of the woods. Then after that if anybody asks you, you're on your way to Taylor Town to buy rations." He shook a finger at the Negro. "Two dollars I'm going to give you if you do just like I say. And if you don't, you better leave this country right then."

"I surely will do my best," the Negro said gravely. "I surely will. Course I never done nothing like this before."

MacSherrill gave a short laugh. "Well, damn me, I never have myself. Anyhow you can keep your mouth quiet."

"Yes, sir."

"I wonder if that scoundrel will run."

"Well, sir, she looks mighty spry to me."

"Keep her warm and dry. Got some chicken for her? Plenty of water. Well." He lingered hanging on the wheel and frowning. "That's Saturday morning at ten. The Kincaid place. And don't let Mr. Tatum or any of his people see you."

"Yes, sir."

"Now," said MacSherrill, "let's go over this one time more."

In the sloping field in front of the Kincaid place it was a gathering of the countryside. Farm horses with trace marks cutting their winter coats, blood horses, their tails banged and something wrong about their legs, half-bred hunters, solemn and able, a calico pony, a couple of mules in blinders, some buggies and old cars.

Up at the columned red brick house Mr. Tatum's Northern visitors watched from the portico, like tourists; ladies in bright knitted dresses, with strings of pearls, stoutish men in golf suits. The last of the riders came out the big front door wiping their mouths and stealing glances at the white butler's morning coat. Mr. Tatum had surely treated everybody well. Even the Negroes were stomping and cackling at the kitchen wing; coffee and doughnuts and a white maid to hand them out. They hushed their fuss as old Colonel Delavan, on his hightailed chestnut saddle horse, came by wriggling his white moustaches and swinging his thin legs in the hooded stirrups. Behind him, driving their fringe-topped surrey, came his second cousins, Miss Fannie, Miss Bella and Miss Chatham Gorrell.

Down the slope MacSherrill hugged the worn saddle with his brown cord breeches and looked down at the pack. That Blue dog showed too many ribs; no way to put meat on him, though, teeth worn down to nubs. Poor old Blue! The hound looked up, sorrowful and deferential, and made a single gesture with his tail. And not only Blue. They all ought to have more flesh, and a shine to their coats. They ought to have a feed of red meat for a change. Hounds couldn't hunt forever on cracklings and corn pudding.

He looked across the pack at Shirley Addison in his stained scarlet coat, his whippy body drawn up in a steeplechase seat, his whipthong hanging down, one eye on the ears of the little old track horse he'd bought at Pimlico, the other on the hounds. Mr. Shirley Addison, gentleman farmer, and dealer in horses among strangers to the neighborhood. He was a good whip, though. His boots were cracked and the tops were almost as black as the rest of the leg. His cap, above his pale reckless face and light brown sideburns, was turning greenish and the bow at the back was worn to a stump. He swung the thong up to his hand and chewed it. He stared at the hounds and at MacSherrill.

"Rad," he gave his pale smile, "that horse going to kill you some day."

"He's got four legs," MacSherrill said. "That's two more than yours."

"Mine's got a head on him," Shirley said; "that's one more than yours. Look coming."

The neat stout figure of Mr. Tatum was riding across the lawn. His dark green English suit was pressed, his black boots shone. The big bright chestnut shook his head against the heavy burnished curb.

"Well, MacSherrill," Mr. Tatum lay back on the reins with iron hands, "what're we going to do today, hey?" His smooth pink face and small blue eyes were confident, obtuse and childlike. "Haven't been doing so much lately, you know. Oh, Addison. Hullo. I promised these good friends of mine I'd show them something," he waved a hand at the porch, the chestnut swung away.

"Look out," MacSherrill said, "that horse is getting in among the hounds."

"That's all right," Mr. Tatum was hearty, "he can take care of himself. Much obliged just the same though. Moggridge!"

"What's that?"

"I guess you boys can stand a little snifter. Might change your luck. Moggridge'll take care of you. Come up here, horse." Boring against the curb the chestnut jogged away.

"Sweet Judas," Shirley Addison said in a low tight voice. His tone cheered up. "Hot damn," he said. "Look coming."

Through the people on the hillside wound the English butler with a silver tray. He stopped unhappily at the edge of the pack while the hounds smelt the striped trousers of his morning coat.

"Never mind me," MacSherrill said. The butler lifted his tray to Shirley. Shirley swallowed the little glass of brandy.

"Hold on, brother," he said; "come back here." The butler came back. Shirley drank MacSherrill's glass. "Rad," he said, "you missed two good drinks. No, one. You never had a chance for mine. Look here," he said, "how come you to meet here today?"

"I told Mr. Tatum I would. You know that."

"There never was a fox in this part of the country."

"Used to be."

Shirley gave his smile. "Expect to find one today?"

MacSherrill pulled a thick gold watch out of his yellow waistcoat pocket. It was time to move off. But he mustn't seem in too big a hurry. He turned the horse with his weight and looked out across the country. The pale washed green of many pastures was broken only by the furry grey of roadside trees and hedgerows and the deep red of winter wheat fields. It was a fine bold open country, big but clean. All you needed was the horse and you could go, with nothing to stop you, to the mountains there against the sky; providing you had a fox. The sky was clear but soft and pearly and there was in the muffled sunlight and in the light breeze, warm and softly moist, a first hint of spring. There ought to be a scent. The hounds were getting restless. They had smelt the crowd and the ground and the butler and found them barren. The warm wind was in their faces and they knew that today if they found a fox they could make him travel.

"Shirley," MacSherrill said, "we'll draw this little woods at the bottom first and then go on down the swamp."

Shirley turned his pale gray eyes to him, looping up the thong of his crop mechanically. "Rad," he said, "there ain't been a fox in there in twenty years."

"Oh well," MacSherrill said, "it'll give the folks something to look at, and settle these hounds down. They're high today." He took up on the reins. Raffle made a quick nip at the bit and then let go. "Look out, pups!" There was a surge away from Rafflle's forelegs. He closed his knees. "Come along, pups."

"Now then, pups," Shirley said in a lifeless voice, "come along." He turned bitter. "It sure will settle them down if we find a rabbit there."

"I'll take the far side," MacSherrill said; "you see that none of them don't drift back up the hill."

At the gate in the fence around the woods he leaned out and unlatched it, too quick and smooth and quiet to give Raffle a chance to rear or swing away. He pushed with his crop handle on the gate. The hounds surged back and then swarmed through beside him. He clamped the cow-horn under his arm and dove into the thicket. "Hi pups, go in! Hi pups, pups, puppies!" They vanished. He worked on into the open woods.

Outside he could hear the voices of the field and the gentle rumble of their horses, and once he heard the crack of Shirley's whip on the hillside and his cold voice. "You, Belle!"

A hound showed now and then in the underbrush, looked at him intently and went on. By now that scoundrel Ezra ought to be in the hilltop woods. He ought to be shaking her out right now. "Hi pups, go in!" But what if she hung a toe in the bag and lamed herself? What if she was lame anyhow? He should have looked. A damn fool trick. "Hi pups!"

Or if she wouldn't run? There was no way of telling that, he'd heard folks say. A dropped fox might do anything. Even squat there till they killed him. Good God Almighty! "Hi pups!"

He was a fool to try it. Why had he bought her? What

good would it do? And to run a risk of being made a fool of. If only she'd run. If she'd run he'd get to their heads and save her. The first good check he'd swing them wrong. Then everybody would be happy. A couple of good miles. That was all he asked. "Hi, pup-pup-puppies!"

Ahead he saw the light at the edge of the woods and the yellow of the swamp. On this side instead of a gate there was a barway with four slip-rails. He didn't want to jump it, he had a notion right at that moment that he might get a fall. He slid to the ground and dropped three rails. The big brown horse would not lead over, he flattened his ears and hung back on the bridle. The son of a —. The dirty —. The lousy —. MacSherrill let the last rail down; the horse walked through.

Back in the saddle, he wished he'd jumped those rails. If the horse had turned over it would have put an end to the whole business. He could have pretended he was hurt. "Hi pups, hi!"

He was on the far side of the swamp now. He could see the stirring of the dead yellow grass and the bare reddish bushes as the hounds worked through it. Across from him in the great big pasture below the Kincaid place the field were watching him. Some of the foot people had come down and the Gorrell girls in their surrey. "Hi pups, push him!" He was in for it now. Well, what of it? These hounds had not had a real good run on fox for three weeks now. They wouldn't work forever on nothing. And he couldn't live forever on nothing either. That feed-bill man would find him. And then they'd all come down on him. He'd have to have some help. And Tatum was the man. A good run was all he needed. One good run right from the place. "Hi, puppies!" He watched the swamp-grass shake as they worked through it. He passed the last trees and was in the open.

Far up the hill below the woods, against the red of the Taylor Town road, he saw a Negro on a mule. That Ezra, right in the road—Good God Almighty. As he looked the figure pointed once across the valley toward the mountains. That damn fool Negro preacher. He picked up the cow-horn from under his arm.

"Hi pups," he blew a single low note and dropped down a bank onto the road where it crossed the swamp. He just dared to steal one more look to the high hill. The Negro on the mule was gone. "Stop 'em, Shirley." His voice was hearty. "Come along, pups."

Black to the bellies, they struggled out of the swamp and fell in behind him, shaking bright mist from their hides. He started up the road toward the high hill. "Come along, pups, come, come!"

When he had reached the big dark unfenced woods above the Kincaid place he turned his horse's head away toward the ridge beyond and stopped him. He waved his hand toward the woods and gave a holler. The pack, flowing behind him on the road, turned off and climbed the bank. He sat still, listening.

There was only the light bustle of the hounds among dead leaves and back on the road the low thump of hooves on clay. Already far along the low side of the woods Shirley's little track horse was lightly galloping. It never took that boy long to get where he belonged. But could they hunt that fox's line? Or if they hit it heel-way and ran it back to where old Ezra had dropped her? And then they'd hit the mule tracks and maybe run them down the road to Taylor Town. And if they ever caught that Negro, stinking of fox, they'd try to eat him and the mule alive. God Almighty!

A high ecstatic quaver—Little Cobweb. And then old Ranter's great coarse moan. He clamped his legs and jumped the bank. The chorus hit him as he ducked the branches. It rolled away from the ridge. He cursed and battled for the lumber road. They had it right and they were moving. Far, far away he heard Shirley's long high scream. He fought with dogwood, beech and sassafras and burst out on the lumber road. Clouting the wet leaves under foot, he heard the jangle of bell notes fly ahead of him. Oh man, but they were running. He swung the horn up and stood in his stirrups. "Wha-wha-wha-wha! Wha-wha-wha-wha!" he blew. A frantic hound, young Redjack, dove from the bushes, flattened his back and raced beside him silently. Far off in open country he heard the faint and trailing cry, "Away-away-away!" Come on, you horse. Did these woods last forever?

In a blaze of sunlight he coasted clear; the great wide scope of valley hit him. Far down the slope, three fields away, he saw the fleck of Shirley's coat and the pack, smooth flowing dots, another field ahead. The brown horse's hocks came under him, he let himself down full blast and took off running at the first low fence. With a shock he landed way down in the field and went to galloping again. More grass. A stone wall and field of pebbly stubble that clung and slowed him. He couldn't gain on them.

In the bottom now he lost them. He stood in his stirrups

and cocked his head to shake the wind of riding from his ears. He couldn't hear them. He rode at a fence between two close-set elms, mean place, and had more grass and a nice wall with a rail on top. He topped a rise of ground and there they were, swinging slowly one field ahead, silent and hunting hard. Shirley was sitting still, his head craned forward, a hand cocked on his hip. A hound spoke. Cobweb again, the little squealy-mouth. They wheeled and started racing.

The fence between them was a double, old rails on both sides of a sunken country lane. The brown horse took a look while he shortened his stride. As he landed he gave a kick at the roadway and dove out the other side through a splintering rail. Shirley's scarlet coat was just going out at the other end. He'd catch them now. He could see them waver and hover in their flight. The brown jumped over the last fence and brought him down a long field spotted with manure. Shirley turned his white face.

"Where you been? See this horse at that double?"

MacSherrill had his cap off as he strode on by. He pointed with it at the manure.

"Don't sit there! Hold 'em on! Come along, pups! Pups! Pups!" Here was a gate; not shut; beyond the grass was clean. "Pups—Pups!" They coasted through around him and spread out at a canter, like a fan; their noses hung below their swinging shoulders. On the left young Redjack turned and started running. He opened—"A-houf-houf!"

"Oh, hark to Redjack! Hark to him, puppies!" Racing they flowed together with whimpers and half choked squeals. "Hi puppies, hi!" They swung to the line, like steel dust to the magnet. They straightened out. The whimpers rose and burst in a jangling torrent. The mottled backs were flowing, trailing shouts and bugles. He whipped the horn up to his puckered mouth. "Wha-wha-wha-wha! Wha-wha-wha-wha!" Oh pups and little bitches, oh flowing speed and music! All that they needed in the whole round world was just a fox to hunt.

They settled to it now and no mistake. He'd show that Shirley a thing or two. Way back he heard the crash of rails. There came the field.

Now they were tied to the line, coasting across the valley. Nothing to do but sit and watch them and let the fences flow beneath his feet. There was a herd of frightened cattle once, and once a field of tender winter wheat and a farmer cursing; a stream with cut-banks, that he floundered through, a man that stood on the roof of his sedan and waved and hollered, and a flight of angry crows against the sky.

The white plank fences of a stock farm, thin and high; between elder bushes, a grass lane, soft green and watery; a stone wall that dropped him on an iron country road. Was that the fringed top of the Gorrells' surrey, galloping? Out of the grass beside the road, over vines and rotten railings and past a stone kitchen and washing on a line. Then two wide open gates and a mile of last year's corn stubs, mean short spikes in mushy loam. At the end, a barway with nice light slip rails. But no time to let them down. The brown got right in under them and went straight up with a twist. You fool, you sorry stinking fool, Whyn't you look, you—Here was a stone wall. You jughead, you can see that, can't you?

He was facing rising ground; the mountains towered above him. In this piece of country the fences had fallen down, there were gaps a'plenty. He could breathe and watch the mottled flying cloud and hear their chime.

As they moved on up through rising pasture lands he kept an eye ahead to see if he could view the fox. They checked abruptly, swung fast all together, hovered, wheeled all together and straightened out. The sweet melodious note was changed, they were chopping it short in fierce hard shouts. The old hounds had turned silent and were moving up in front. They knew. He looked ahead and caught a fleck of red that vanished over a ridge. He took a hold of Raffle; they were going to catch that fox. His fingers slacked off. Just before she made the mountains where she came from.

The cry stopped. The pack had shut their mouths and were racing up a rocky shoulder. Now he could see her. Ahead like a sick red cat she was dragging; her muzzle hung, her mouth was open, she hooked herself along with hunched high shoulders, her wet brush and her dead legs trailed behind. She reached the far end and crawled through the bottom of a boundary fence. While the silent pack were flowing over the top rails she crept on steadily up a long stumpy pasture.

At a stump she turned and gave a little high scream. The flat hard-running pack rolled over her.

He took a pull on Raffle: high rails against the light. High rails right up the hill and beyond, in the stumpy ground, the frantic pack that tugged and fought with bitter growls. Then at the last he kicked him. The big horse dropped his head and raised his giraffe withers into MacSherrill's face—bang! bang!

It was right around his loins, the knives and fire, the sickening gnawing of the pulp. He'd vomit if he dared. He smelt a sharp aroma, the hounds, stinking of fox, were sniffing at him. Far off he heard Shirley's voice, small and cold. "You hounds, keep back there!" The voice came closer, "Rad, can you hear me? Don't try to move. You lay still till Doc Beasly comes."

The dark mountains loomed, the gray sky weighed him down. He was trapped and mangled in a dark world. And it was cold. He felt Shirley laying his own old scarlet coat on top of him.

Here came the veterinary on the patched-up Gold Cup horse and the pig-tailed girl on the horse no one would ride. He could hear the others coming and the whistle of Cap'n Longstreth's windy gray.

Behind him he heard a voice, "Mister MacSherrill, are you hurt?" He brought his eyes back to a focus. The pain made a hard bright lens through which he saw, sharp and huge, Mr. Tatum, the Northern man. His hat was dented and his English riding suit was red with clay. A thorn scratch marked his smooth pink face, radiant with a child-like trembling smile. He was almost crying. "Are you all right?"

He took what breath he dared and made his voice sound strong. "Just fine, Mr. Tatum."

"Thank God, Mister MacSherrill," he took MacSherrill by the hand. "This is the finest day of my life, my friend. Yes sir, the greatest day. Never knew hunting could be anything like this. Yes sir, this settles it. Say, are you all right?"

Once more he wrestled with his tight dead chest. The words came out. "Just fine."

"Good. That's good. Well sir, this settles it. It looks like I was going to stay right here for keeps."

"That would be mighty nice." The words were loud, tremendous; they crashed above the ringing in his ears.

Mr. Tatum laid a hand on his shoulder. "Oh, excuse me. I guess that's kind of tender. But look here. It may not be the time to mention it. But I guess there's always the cost of everything to think of." Mr. Tatum turned red. "Well, I don't know the rules and I don't want to butt in. You know. But I'm no piker either. I want to do my share."

"Well that's mighty nice, Mr. Tatum."

"Just say the word, friend. There's only one thing I ask. I'd like to count on having you meet at my place every Lincoln's birthday." He started to give MacSherrill's shoulder a pat, then took his hand down. "A great day. I want to make it an anniversary."

"Shirley," MacSherrill held his belly tight and made the words with care, "you got the brush? Bring it here. Mr. Tatum," he said, "I'd be mighty pleased if you'd hang that over your fireplace."

"Great governor," Mr. Tatum took off his punctured hat. "I never expected anything like this." He took the chewed wet brush in his hands and stared at it like a crystal gazer. MacSherrill turned his sick eyes to the hounds. He had surely gotten away with murder. He looked at the stump where the vixen had made her stand —murder.

On the road he heard more horses coming. He made out the gait of the Colonel's saddle horse and the heavy feet of Uncle Dunc's half percheron. There were low calls and murmurs and the wheels of the Gorrell girls' surrey, galloping. They were around him now. More coats came over him, he heard them mutter. "Damn. That Yankee pestering him . . . Rad, take it easy . . . don't you move."

He heard a laboring motor and the bang of an auto door. Then he could smell the cigars in Doc Beasly's vest. Far off, more words. Oh, God, why did they always have to talk?

"How is he, doc?"

"Doc, that horse rolled right clean over him."

"Sure did. And then rolled back and lay on him."

Doc Beasly stood up. "Get me my bag. Whose Ford is that? Well, you drive into town and get the ambulance. Much obliged, son."

A bag clicked open. Little bottles clinked. Doc Beasly rummaged in the bag. "Now hold still, son." He felt the stubby, fumbling hands and then the sharp sting of the needle. He licked his lips. They were caked and sour. Above, the mountains stood up dark and heavy. Beyond his feet, the grass was torn up around the stump and there was a scrap of fur.

It was flowing through him now, a tide of thin soft numbness from Doc Beasly's needle. He worked his lips to loosen them.

"Give me some more of that stuff, Doc," he said. "I feel so mean."

Shiftless

How I came to know Abijah Peabody and Fred was this. I'd gone into Beauregard with Uncle Duncan to get some cotton ginned. They were teams ahead of us, so we went down to watch the shoofly train come in. Dogs were more plentiful than usual round the station that day and niggers about average, though one of them played an accordion, which is something most niggers can't catch on to. They was a hound eating train-oil off the ties, and Uncle Duncan offered to bet me five cents to a quarter that the shoofly'd run him down. But I knew he was a regular station hound, so I didn't. And, sure enough, when he heard the rails jig he hopped off the track and went into the grocery store.

When the train came in, a little old man bounded off it, looking every way, quick, like a turkey. He had a stiff suit and a stiff collar and a stiff hat. His face was round, but his nose was pointed.

He saw me, and came up, stepping fast. "Young man," he said—and I knew he was Northern—"I'll give ye ten cents to fetch my grip out."

"Call him 'son,' " Uncle Duncan said, "and he'll do it for nothing."

But I was kind of insulted, so I just said, "Why, Mister, they's plenty niggers round here."

So he went up to the nearest one, a yellow nigger named Will, that works in the poolroom. And what do you think? He called him "young man."

He hustled back to the car with Will and they came out with two big bags. He was talking and fussing over his shoulder at Will. Behind them was a tall, gangling young fellow about my age. He had his hands in his pockets and slouched along, kind of edgewise. At first I thought he didn't belong to the old man, and I reckon that's what he aimed to make folks think. But the old fellow noticed he was falling behind and called back, "Come on, Fred! We're going to the hotel." The old man headed for the hotel, carrying one bag and helping Will with the other. The one he called Fred came easing along after him. As he passed me he grinned kind of sheepish and jerked his head toward Will.

"Another nigger ruined," he said, and went on down the street.

The train waited there a little while because the engineer had to see Sheriff McNeill about a setter pup, and the sheriff was late on account of the shoofly being on time. I went over to look at the pup, and pretty soon Sheriff McNeill came along, and after considerable chat he gave the engineer five dollars for him. It was a good pup, though.

The train pulled out then, and Uncle Duncan and I went back to the gin.

Well, sir, we found that old fellow had come all the way from Maine to take hold of the old Vaughan place. His wife had been one of the heirs, and when she died she left her husband her share. He'd met her when she was a girl in Charleston and he was on a coasting-schooner. So before she died she got him to buy out the other heirs and promise to come down to run the place. They'd sent their boy to State College; that was the young fellow, Fred.

I saw Fred again the very next day when I came in town. He was sitting on a bench in front of the poolroom, betting with a fellow on the age of every mule that was tied up to the railings. They were playing for twenty-five cents a year; that is, for every year the mule was old. Fred was sitting with his hat pulled down over his eyes and his legs spread out. He could sit to look more like a fellow lying down than any man ever I saw. They were smoking and counting their money because they'd bet on all the mules there. Just then a farmer drove up with another.

"Sixteen," said Fred.

"Twelve," said the other fellow.

"Hi, Brother!" Fred said; "how old that mule?"

"I don't know," the farmer said; "I bought him last year for twelve."

"Look at his teeth," Fred said to the other fellow.

The other fellow looked at his teeth. " 'Bout thirteen," he said.

Fred said, "Here you are," and he handed him seventy-five cents.

"Well, I must be going," the fellow said, and went off down the street.

Fred saw me then, and must have remembered the evening before because he said, "Hi, Brother, how you?"

"Fine," I said, and I sat down alongside him.

"Who was that fellow?" he said.

"I don't know. Stranger," I told him. "I wouldn't trust these yer strangers," I said.

"I don't," he said, "but it's a mighty warm evening to go messing with a mule's teeth for seventy-five cents.

"My old man," he went on, "is exerting himself powerfully to-day. He's fixing to move out to that place to-morrow. He sent me after some groceries."

"Did you get them all right?" I asked him.

"Why, no," he said, looking kind of surprised. "I'm waiting for them now," and he settled down on the bench.

But just then I heard a tap-tapping coming down the pavement, and there come old man Peabody, same gait as usual.

I turned round to tell Fred. But he was gone.

When I saw Fred next time I asked him if he'd gotten the groceries.

"You know," he said, "they hadn't taken as long to wrap 'em up as I'd expected. Dad, though, appeared to think there had been some kind of lack of industry on my part. He gets those ideas about everybody. He naturally loves to fly around. And I naturally don't."

"Why, no," I said. " 'Course not."

"Up in New England, though," Fred said, "where Dad comes from, that's the way folks acts. When I was a boy Dad'd whip me if he caught me sitting round."

"At home," I said, "Uncle Duncan gets oneasy unless I am sitting round. He expects I'm up to some devilment."

"Yes, I know," he said; "that's the way my mother was; she was Southern, and I reckon I taken after her."

"You don't favor your paw," I said.

"You know," he said, "Dad and I don't make out very

good together. I wish we could. He's more less lonely now. But he wastes all his time running round. Only he thinks I waste all mine sitting still. I'll be glad to go back to school next week. I'm studying agriculture, and they's a good job waiting for me in the Spring when I get through."

I didn't see him again before he left, but we can make out the Vaughan place from ours, and we used to watch what Abijah Peabody was doing there. First thing, he hired a couple of niggers and put everything out of the house and washed that house all over the inside. Folks said he even washed the walls, and one of the niggers told it round town that he washed the ceilings. Uncle Duncan reckoned the old man had got the idea that Squire Vaughan had died of some catching complaint. We all knew the squire had naturally drunk hisself to death, so Uncle Duncan went over in a friendly way to tell the old man he had no call to take all that trouble. I went along.

Sure enough, Abijah was scrubbing the wall in the parlor.

Uncle Duncan said, "Good evening," and Abijah just said "Good afternoon," and went right on. Uncle Duncan is mighty slow to get insulted, so he didn't pay any attention. He just said:

"I saw you washing the house, and I thought maybe you had the idea there was some catching complaint hereabouts, but you needn't be uneasy; they isn't any such thing."

Abijah turned hisself round in that quick way, and he said:

"Friend"—I never heard "friend" said so unfriendly—

"Friend," he said, "when I want any help here I'll ask for it. I'm going to have a clean house if it's the only one in North Carolina."

"The folks round here," Uncle Duncan said, "are mighty neighborly. They will be pleased to know that you are not too proud to ask assistance when you require it," and he walked away. The old man stared after him like he couldn't make him out. I expect he'd never seen any folks like Uncle Duncan before.

The next thing Abijah did was to paint. He painted everything in sight, and when it looked like there was nothing else to do he got him a barrel of whitewash and started to whitewash the trees in the apple orchard. Folks used to stop along the road to watch him doing it. But none of them went in because they had the idea that he was a right mean old fellow. The two niggers quit him 'count of everybody laughing at them for having to whitewash trees. The white folks told them that Abijah was going to make them whitewash his mules when they got done with the trees. They looked solemn at those niggers and said they'd heard tell it was sure death to whitewash a mule's tail.

Abijah didn't whitewash his mules, but he brushed them every day. He said at the post office it was good for them. He was a curious man.

Yes, sir, he was curious. He used to hold forth at the post office all the time. He said he'd come down to farm because he knew what Southerners was like, and figured that if they could make a living here a Yankee that knew how to work could make a fortune.

"Why," he said, "I've only been here a month and look at my house."

"I have," Uncle Duncan said, "often. What about your house?"

Abijah's face got red and his eyes popped out.

"Why," he says, "it's painted."

"And in two years the sun will peel the paint off. What will you do then?"

"I don't believe that," the old man said, "but if it does I'll paint her again, by gosh!"

Uncle Duncan shook his head. "A waste of time."

I thought Abijah would bust right out of his hide.

"It preserves the wood," he hollered; "anybody knows that!"

"The old Vaughan place has stood without paint for a hundred years. It is just as stout as the day it was built. Heart pine needs no paint; it is full of rosin. You are wasting your time."

"Wasting my time! Great Land A'mighty, I guess I've done more in the last two months than you have in a year."

"What have you done? Considerable work—mostly useless. But you have made no friends."

Abijah just said, "Huh." He stood there puffing hisself and turning his little beak here and yon, and began to talk about Maine, cutting his words off short like a fodder-chopper.

"Where I come from," he said, "every house is painted white, with a white barn built right onto it, handy."

Some one asked him if that didn't make the flies bad in Summer.

"No, siree," he said, "we don't have any flies in Maine, nor loafers either."

"Nor Summer, I reckon," the same fellow said.

But Abijah kept on: "We wouldn't keep a hired man

ten minutes that hung back on us the way you let these colored fellers do. What they need is a feller from down East to handle them."

I almost laughed. He went right on to talk about the South then, about how we all were shiftless and fooled away our time and let the niggers do all the work and didn't make them do it right.

Uncle Duncan listened for a while. Then he smiled and said to Abijah, "Why do you spend your time trying to change the natural order? It does not appear to make you happy."

"Happy!" Abijah said, "I wasn't raised to be happy. I was raised to work!" He walked up and down, looking mighty angry. "That's what worries me about my boy Fred. That boy's mother made me send him down here to school, to State College, and what I always said would happen has happened. The boy's got shiftless. He talks slow and drawling. He loafs round when he's home. He never gets excited about anything except dancing and drinking and going hunting. My folks was brought up hard and they worked hard. There's never been a shiftless man or woman in the Peabody family yet, and now there's going to be one—all on account of my foolishness. You'd think he was a Southerner, bred and born."

"I trust, sir, you are mistaken," Uncle Duncan said, "for if he has become a Southerner it will make him very uncomfortable in your presence."

"I guess I'll make him more uncomfortable than he does me," Abijah said, with a little dry laugh like a fox-bark. And he walked out with the idea he had got the best of Uncle Duncan.

He got some other niggers to take the place of the two who left, and explained to them what ailed the white folks round here. He told them that he believed a man should take niggers into his confidence. The niggers said that was so, and came and asked Uncle Duncan if they should work for Abijah any more. Uncle Duncan said, "Yes."

So they did. But they were uneasy. Abijah explained everything to them. Then he argued with them. Then he got mad and did the work hisself while they stood and watched him. After so long a time those two niggers found he couldn't handle them and they became mighty resentful toward him.

Abijah couldn't make out what was the trouble; he'd spend a hour proving to the niggers how he was right and they was wrong. And at the end they'd just skulk off, looking sideways. The more he proved to those niggers the less he got out of them.

I was going to town one morning, and I saw Abijah and the niggers clearing some new ground. They had the mules and a stump puller. Abijah was waving his arms at the niggers, and they were kind of shifting round. When he saw me he came down to the fence arunning. I started to say good morning, but he cut right in. "Say, young man," he said, "going to town?"

I said I was.

"Coming back soon?"

I said I aimed to.

"Well, here's the ratchet to my stump puller," he said; "it's broke. I told those durn colored men there was four thousand pounds came on the pin if they let go, but they won't listen to a thing I say. Take it in and get me another."

So I took it. As I went off he said, "Obliged," but it came out harder than any stump in his new ground.

When I got to town I found a new ratchet cost three dollars and a half, but the man in the garage said he'd weld me the old one for fifty cents if I'd wait. So I did, and he sure made a job.

I got back along about evening. Abijah came stepping down to the fence. I started to tell him how I'd saved him three dollars, but he shouted, "Saved me three dollars! Land of Mercy! I been waiting for that ratchet since ten o'clock this morning! I've lost a whole day—and what about the niggers and the mules?—my time's worth five dollars a day if it's worth a nickel."

"Why, Mister," I said, "they isn't nobody's time worth five dollars a day. I aimed to save you money."

"You're like the rest of them," he said; "don't know the value of time. You've got no sense. Listen here; I can always get more money, but I can't get back this day."

I knew I had him then, so I just laughed. "Why, Mister Peabody," I said, "I got a five-dollar bill home and I declare I don't know where to get another. But days," I said, "why, man, I got all the days they is."

He just looked at me a minute like I was some kind of curious animal. Then he grabbed up the package and went up to the barn.

When I told Uncle Duncan he got right mad because the old man cussed me after I'd obliged him. He didn't say anything, but the next evening he was in town he ran into Abijah at the post office. The old fellow was blowing off about what ailed the South. Uncle Duncan listened to the end, then he said, "Peabody, do you know what ails you? I have seen several Yankees in the South and I know; you are all the same. You come down here and treat the niggers like white folks and the white folks like niggers. And both despise you."

The old man didn't answer this time. He was kind of taken back. I reckon he'd got the idea that Uncle Duncan was soft because he was polite.

One night, not long before Christmas, I was out back of the house fixing up my possum-dog. He'd cut hisself in a stock-fence the day before and I was greasing him. After I got through he rolled in the dirt like a dog does and then he started toward the branch and looked back. The moon was up, and it was a pretty night to catch a possum. The sycamores showed as white as corpses. No wonder the niggers is scared of them. Across the branch you could see the old Squire Vaughan place all painted up, standing out as bright as day. It was an old, old house, and used to kind of fit into the country like the other old houses round, but now it didn't appear to belong there any more than Abijah Peabody hisself. I stood there studying about him. He sure was a great man to work and to fix up everything. He despised shiftlessness. And yet if we all was to become like him, I expect we'd all be worse off.

The dog was snuffing around in the bushes, and I was half listening to him and half thinking about old man Peabody. Just then I heard some one turn in our road, walking fast, and I thought it must be Abijah, but it was Fred.

"Hi," I said, "when did you get back from school?"

"I just got in on Number Two," he said; "want to go coon-hunting?"

"Yes, sir," I said, "and let me tell you, boy, right yer, I got the coon-huntingest dog in this county." And I pointed down to the branch where old Rattler was bumballing round.

"I know," he said; "everybody has. Call your dog."

"Wait till I get a ax."

"Don't need a ax," he said. "I got those two niggers of Dad's and they each got a tree-dog, and I got two axes and matches; everything's in good fix. Come on."

I whistled to Rattler and we went down the road to where the niggers was. The big one, Ance, had a blue-ticked bitch, and Jim, the little nigger, had a little red fyst. When we got down near the big swamp the dogs left us, and we sat down on a hill. We sat for a hour or maybe two and never heard a sound except now and then one of the dogs crackling through the dead cane. We were bout ready to move when 'way down the branch I heard old Rattler open, "Ou—ou—ou!" Then there came a "Ki—i, ki—i," and Jim jumped up: "Hi—i—i, you! Das mah lil' red dawg." Then for a while we couldn't hear anything, then it sounded nearer, then further away. Then all of a sudden they bustled loose right down the hill, all three. Ance jumped up: "Hiiiiii! Big Blue!"

"They're getting a close race on him!" Fred said. "Now you niggers, listen!"

The noise died off a minute, and then they come back hollering fit to jar the ground. "A sight-race!" Fred said. "Come on, boys; they'll tree him sure!" The little nigger tripped on the top of the hill and rolled clear out of sight. We took out down the grade aflying and left him. As we hit the branch we heard them tonguing long and deep, like clockwork. "Treed!" said Fred. "Come on, boys!" There he was, sure enough, up a sweet gum and all three dogs trying to throw themselves over the top of it. Ance started to chop, but he was plumb blowed out.

"Here, give me the ax," Fred said, and began knocking chips half-way across the branch. Jim come up with water running out of his ears, and about then the sweet gum came down. They was a pile of niggers and dogs and branches, and a dead coon at the bottom. We built a fire, and Fred had a half a quart of monkey-rum to keep us warm. Everybody lied about their dogs and told about coon-hunts and fox-chases, and 'long about three, when the moon got low, we went home.

Rattler didn't come back, so next morning I went over to the Vaughan place to see if he was there with the niggers' dogs. I found him, and started home. I didn't want to run into Fred's dad. But that scoundrel dog kept hanging back on the string I had tied round him. I reckon he had the idea of courting the blue bitch. I made poor time, and the old man saw me. He called me back to the barnyard, where he was with Fred.

"You were hunting with my boy last night?" he said.

"Yes, sir," I said; "we sure had a pretty race. Old Rattler yer—"

"I don't want to hear about it," he said. "My boy comes home from college with more to do on this place than three could do and the first night he has to go off hunting with you and the colored hands."

"But the niggers each had a dog—we couldn't have made out without them. And niggers naturally love to coon-hunt."

"He knew I told those hands I wanted them on the place at night. And what happened? He goes off with them against my orders, and the brown mule gets cast in her stall, and now to-day she's lame so I can't pull stumps in the new ground."

"I expect my uncle could lend you a mule," I said.

"It ain't the mule that riles me," he said; "it's seeing a son of mine so shiftless he'd rather lower himself going hunting with colored men than stay home and tend to business."

Fred got mad then: "You needn't to be so busy about my lowering myself, Dad," he said. "I hunted with them last night, but this morning I'm still white, and they know it—better than you, it appears like." He looked like he felt mighty bad.

"I don't want any sass!" Abijah said. "Now you two listen here—" he turned to me. "I won't have you hunting any more with my boy." Then he turned to Fred: "And you—I want you to keep away from those hands. I hire them and I'll handle them. You've nothing to do with them. Is that clear?"

Well, of course, I kept away from the Vaughan place after that. But the week after the New Year Fred came in about suppertime. I knew he was going back to school, and thought he had come to tell me good-by.

"Yes," he said, "I'm due to go to-morrow. But I'm in more or less a fix right now."

I asked him the trouble.

"Why," he said, "you know how Dad is. Well, the other day he was talking to the niggers about the mules. He told them a long story about people not feeding mules right. That what a mule needed was feed with a high potash content to make him stout. He said, as far as I can make out, that corn and pea-vine hay had no potash and that oats was better on that account. Well, the niggers figured that they'd please Dad by putting a power of potash into those mules, so the next time they mixed the oats with fertilizer and both mules like to died. The old man ran those niggers off the place without paying them their wages. He told me he'd explained everything to them and it was their own fault. That's the way he is about things.

"Well, this evening I went into town for the mail. I started playing cowboy-pool with some fellow, and all the time Will, that poolroom nigger, kept looking at me mighty solemn. It made me so nervous I lost five dollars, so at the end I told Will he'd have to save up and pay me back or else take his eyes off me. But he just waited till the other boys had gone, and then he told me that those two niggers that worked for Dad was telling it round to the others that they were coming out to-night to get their money. They said Dad had cheated them, and doggone me if I don't think they're right, they being niggers.

"Anyhow I gave Will a quarter, and came right on out. I stopped in to ask if you'd come on over and help me out in case they come round."

"I sure will," I said. "I can take care of one," I said, "and you take the other."

"Oh," he said, "I don't want you to take care of any

nigger, I want you to take care of Dad. Dad's liable to get hisself shot up, the way he carries on."

So I went along with Fred.

He had a room in the back of the house. The walls were painted yellow and the ceiling blue. I never saw such a room. Everything in it was just so. On the walls he had pictures.

We could hear the old man moving upstairs, going to bed. Fred looked up at the ceiling, then he looked at me.

"You know," he said, "I don't know what to do about that old fellow."

"Looks like he can't make out down here," I said. "Maybe he'd do better in Maine, where he understands more about things."

"He sure would," said Fred; "but he can't go back."

I began studying whether the folks there had run him out or what. Fred must have known it because he went on:

"You see, he put everything he had into buying this place like he promised my ma he would. He had to borrow money, too, only he never told her. Yes, sir, he's naturally bound down to this farm."

"Uncle Duncan would have helped him," I said. "Only you can't do anything for him, it appears like."

"Nobody can help him," Fred said. "He can always prove he's right."

After so long a time everything was quiet up-stairs, and Fred spread a blanket on the floor. I asked him if that was for me.

"Why," he said, "it's for both of us," and he took a hand out of his pocket and rolled a pair of dice down that blanket just as soft and easy, just a little twist, but those bones kept on arolling like they'd never stop.

"Hicks an' a three," he says. "Dice me, boy; I'm a dicing man," and I could see he was.

He put out the lamp, and we shaded a candle so that no light showed outside, and we settled down to play.

I don't know how long we played there, whispering, so as not to wake up Fred's dad. It must have been a hour or two. I doubled three times and lost, and Fred reached forward his hand to take in the money. Instead he held it there for a minute, looking over his shoulder, then he nipped the candle out. We sat there listening. The next room was Abijah's office, and I could just make out little, soft movements in there. As my eyes got used to the dark I saw a dim light under the door. Fred started to get on his feet very easy and I did too, but when I was halfway up one of my knee joints gave an awful crack like they sometimes do. Something dropped in the next room with a bang, and then we heard Abijah's feet hit the floor over our heads and run to the top of the stair.

Next thing we heard him squeak, "Who's that?" Then he must have seen them because he piped out, "Get out of this house, I tell you, or I'll have the law on yer. By gosh, I will!"

Then one of the niggers said, "Jim and me come fo' our money."

You could tell by his voice that he was just scared enough to do something foolish, and Fred opened the door.

There they were in the hall, Abijah was on the stair with a flashlight wabbling all over the place. The niggers each had tied a handkerchief round their face, though anyone could tell them from the back of their head. The big one had an old-time pistol, kind of dangling from his hand.

Fred went up to him and said, "Hello, Ance; that gun of yours is half cocked; it won't go off like it is. Give it here." Ance handed him the gun. "What you and Jim doing here?"

"We come fo' our money, Mistah Fred," Ance said.

"Well, you won't get it coming this away," Fred said. "You'll get the road gang."

The niggers shuffled around.

Fred went on, "I aimed to have you two arrested for poisoning those mules."

" 'Deed, Mistah Fred," the one called Ance said, "we didn't go to poison no mule."

Then the little one said, "We des aimed to please yo' paw, Mist' Fred; 'fo' God, dasso."

"Well, what about sneaking into this house and these yer handkerchiefs and gun?" Fred said.

Each of them looked at the other nigger like he was trying to blame him for getting him into this.

Then Jim says, "Ance' o' woman got de 'sumption."

" 'Tain't de 'sumption," Ance said; "it's de miasma. De doctor say to git aigs. I figured on de money for de aigs."

"Whyn't you keep chickens?"

"Why, Mist' Fred, you know 'tain't no use with de san' fleas an' all these yer South Carolina niggers movin' in."

Fred had been looking at the gun. "Why," he says, "this gun ain't loaded."

"No, suh," Ance said; "I ain't foolin' round with no live

bullets in de dark. No, suh. De gun was des fo' a decoy. Ah des aimed to git mah wages to git aigs. De o' woman cough an' cough—"

"Here," Fred says, "you come with me."

He led them out to the back porch. I heard him say, "Hold out your hat, Ance." Then some eggs dropped into it.

"Mist' Fred, suh," Ance said, "de Lord will so'ly bless you."

"I don't know about that," Fred said, "but if ever I catch you two niggers round this place I'm going to nail both your black hides up on this yer siding."

"Yessuh, dasso," they both said, and began blessing him again.

"Now, travel," Fred said, and I could hear them shuffle off the porch. He came back into the hall.

Old man Peabody stumbled down the stairs; his face was all kind of fallen down and his chin trembled.

"Fred," he said, "I don't know how to treat 'em, and that's a fact."

Fred got kind of embarrassed; he began clicking the dice together. He'd had them in his hand all the while. I saw the old man look at him right hard, but he didn't say a thing. After a while Fred rolled them out on the table and read them kind of absent. He swept the bones away and turned round toward his Dad.

"You know," he said, "I reckon I won't go back to school."

Fred came by next day.

"You sure enough going to stay on the farm?" I asked him.

"Yes, sir," he said, "Dad was mighty nice this morning. He offered me a third of the crops."

"Well, that's good," I said; "only you know, Fred, I feel kind of bad about those niggers. Good niggers is scarce. It's a pity you had to lose them."

"Oh," he said, "when I got up this morning, first thing I saw was those two niggers working down in the new ground, grubbing stumps."

The Flat Town

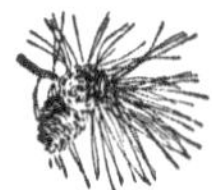

IN the middle of the flat coastal plain, Central Junction stuck up, rigid and incongruous. The town seemed to have been dropped into the heart of the gray, motionless seas from the blue, unwinking sky. Its uniformity was, however, Southern rather than celestial; all streets were straight, parallel and equidistant; all stores had flat roofs and pressed-brick fronts; all houses, concrete walks and golden oak front doors; all churches, magenta stained-glass windows and fret-sawed porticos.

The citizens of Central Junction were uniform. They could not be distinguished from the citizens of any small town, nor even from each other. Nothing marked the individual save imperceptibly fine shades of relative obscurity. Central Junction had no drunks, no Catholics, no Jews, no beauty, and no brains, and it contemplated all these deficiencies with equal complacency.

Of this primitive tribal village, Mr. Wilmer Scabes was head man. He had lived there all his life. It was, he often said, good enough for him. And neither he, with a webbed hand spread impressively on his slack paunch, nor his ring of moon-faced auditors caught any glimmer of the dreadful implication.

His life moved in a fixed orbit between his chocolate-colored residence and his rectangular grocery. Though he held no office, the heavy power of his righteousness controlled the town. On his solemn daily round he often paused to dispense weather remarks and aphorisms among such citizens as crossed his churning bows, then passed on, a stately caravel freighted with great thoughts, and left their shallow minds whirling like midges in his wake. At such times his formless face and body radiated a faint and heatless effulgence as does the firefly by day. And like the firefly's, the emanation was purely mechanical.

Small wonder that twenty years' leadership of Central Junction's uncolored life had made his graciousness both conscious and perfunctory. Not that Mr. Scabes was discontent; on the contrary, he was buoyed by the knowledge of his rectitude, knowledge as precise as his monthly statement of bills receivable. If there were greater happiness than this, he often told himself, he had not heard of it. And yet his light blue eyes, even in the midst of weighty affairs, would sometimes leave the speaker's face and gaze disconsolately afar. They narrowed and brightened with a flash of unguessed fire, as though seeking new horizons. Their lustre swiftly faded as they met nothing but the flat town and the flat fields beyond.

They wandered even now as Mr. Scabes stood on the street discussing the new waterworks with Mr. Podginson, the mayor. He heard Mr. Podginson's dry, windy voice:

"Men to put up the reservoir tank came today. Don't like their looks; hard young fellers; ain't done nothing out of the way yet, but I reckon they will."

He heard no more, though he was just conscious of the

continued vibration of Mr. Podginson's chin-whiskers and of his melancholy reiteration, "wa'erworks—wa'erworks" like the harsh cry of some persistent and idiotic fowl. Mr. Scabes was not listening, not even thinking. He was just slipping away for an instant from Mr. Podginson, from town affairs, from his own level life of fifty years. He did this often of late and it worried him. A man at his age, a leading citizen, should settle down. All his people had been well thought of; all except that woman his grandfather had married, Jacqueline, her name was, heathenish or papish.

"Here they come now," Mr. Podginson was prodding him with a meagre elbow.

"Who? Oh! Ah!"

Three youths in jumpers lounged with calculated unconsciousness along the sidewalk. Each had a cap of extreme design raked over one eye and a cigarette cocked in the corner of a saturnine mouth. As they passed, one indicated Mr. Podginson by a nod and murmured, "Uncle Joshuay" in an explanatory tone. Mr. Podginson turned on them a cold and outraged eye and encountered three dry grins.

It was clear that these youths boded Central Junction no good.

And yet at first their behavior was passably restrained. Wilmer Scabes, as in duty bound, stepped out daily to watch their progress. Each morning he took up a position at a dignified distance and gazed upon them with a mien which he conceived to be benevolently austere. They gathered their material, plates, beams, kegs of rivets and tackle on the ground in admirable professional silence marred only by an unnecessarily aggressive technique in expectoration. They watched the local concrete man pour the footings with sombre, fixed stares, offensive chiefly in what they might leave unexpressed.

But as the superstructure rose and they with it, their spirits rose as well. And they were not spirits of a sort which commended themselves to Wilmer Scabes.

Sitting in his grocery, he could hear the hammering of the rivets, the crash of I-beams and occasional shouts. As the work proceeded, the character of these shouts became clear. They were oaths and scandalous epithets. They rang through the drowsy grocery, more resonant, more impious, more shameless each day that the three hard young men mounted nearer Heaven. And, looking out of the window, Mr. Scabes saw that every word fell plummeting like an obscene bird of prey upon the shrinking town. Housewives passed, grim virtue on their blanched, adamantine faces, and an alert ear cocked to the skies for the three youths' strange blasphemies. Two church members, their bulging eyes upcast, stood transfixed at the sound of familiar words in unbelievable juxtaposition. Horace, the grocery boy, shut off the engine of the delivery car and listened with a scared grin. Mr. Scabes cleared his resounding throat ominously and cast on Horace a baleful look. The grin vanished, Horace cranked her fervently and drove off.

The character of the three erecting men was manifest. Mr. Scabes gave up visiting the water tower. A man in his position could not afford to stand in the presence of evil. The waterworks for which he had striven had long since become distasteful and he would have been glad of a reason to dismiss them. He was disturbed to find, however, that instead of welcoming the chance to do so he now felt a horrid attraction towards the scene of this loud and forbidden dialogue. Though powerfully reinforced by his sense of moral rectitude, he missed his daily visit more and more. He even found degrading solace in the fact that entire escape from contamination was impossible. For there was in Central Junction no haven from the pervasive and ringing indecencies of the three youths poised above it. They penetrated the utmost recesses of Central Junction and of Mr. Scabes' grocery.

At the Wednesday prayer meeting he pressed his brow against the back of the pew in front of him and fixed his eyes on the intricate vermicelli pattern of the red carpet. He was framing his thoughts in ponderous phrases. Standing up, he regarded through half-closed lids the rows of black backs inclined in prayer, then lifted a sonorous voice to supplicate that the godless strangers now in their midst might be led into paths of grace. He sat down to the approving rustle of bombazine. A hymn followed: "Rescue the Perishing." He was the leader of the singing. In preparation he drew his chin into his white bow tie and expanded his gills like a cobra about to strike. Then in a ringing baritone of great power, he hit the first note with deadly accuracy and swung the docile congregation into the tune.

On his way home, he passed the three unregenerates, propped negligently against the drugstore, whistling a vulgar melody through their teeth. The swing of their music quickened his unwilling steps. In the quiet side street the whistling sounded faint and died away. He walked more slowly, rejoicing that he had never used his own voice save in the service of the Lord.

The sinful trio were now a charge upon his conscience. He tended the grocery absently, his well-lobed ears on wait for the next impiety to float in through the door. The toll grew; not a corroding syllable was forgotten. Worse than the actualities were the shouts and snatches of song whose words were lost in a gust of wind or a clash of steel. Upon such obscurities the anxious Mr. Scabes spent hours of horrid conjecture.

The tower mounted higher. The three hard youths, swinging toward the sky like demigods, cast off magnificently all restraint. The sober rat-tat of their pneumatic riveters gave place to barbarous rhythms of their own design; they executed double shuffles on the precarious footways; they halooed unspeakable indecencies to each other across the void; they joined uproariously in songs of coarse mirth.

The sheet steel sections of the tank itself, like huge black orange peels, were hoisted up and riveted together. Within this ringing bowl the three celestial scalawags abandoned themselves to song.

They sang, "She's a Rose with a Broken Stem," and other tender ballads. They sang, most scandalously, "Pull For the Shore, Sailor," with a double syncopated accompaniment of pneumatic jacks. They sang, "The Captain Went Below" and the lurid, "Hot Boy." And then at the close of day they executed a voluntary or fanfare on the riveters, followed by a long, harmonious "O-o-o-o-h" which fixed the attention of the pavid and expectant town.

"O-o-o-o-h" they sang, "She-e-e-e ripped and she snorted and she rolled on the floor—" and right on through to the outrageous and unspeakable climax. They ended with a defiant, "tat-tiddy-tat-tat—tat-tat" of the hammers and quit work.

As the days went on, this unvarying evening song became for Mr. Scabes a sort of diabolic angelus. When the hour approached he stopped work and anxiously took a post of vantage. Then came the long "O-o-o-o-h." He pursed his lips; but his eyes were bright. Across the street, Mr. Podginson raised his distracted whiskers to the sky. Throughout the town, indoors and out, the citizens remained with rigid faces and straining eyes till the last note died away.

One evening as the familiar final "tat-tiddy-tat-tat" sounded, Mr. Scabes, at the grocery door, was swaying toe and heel to the rhythm. He became conscious of Mr. Podginson's astonished eye and hastily withdrew. He had made himself ridiculous and even under suspicion before Mr. Podginson. He would be much better occupied in bringing the three pagan mechanics to a conviction of sin than in shuffling his feet to their flaunting song. He would sternly check this insult to Central Junction, too long endured; he would show them there was one place where ribaldry could not lift its head. And he would place himself in the right light with Mr. Podginson.

At five o'clock next afternoon when, high above the town, Satan's chorus was swelling to full power, Wilmer Scabes approached the watertank with Mr. Podginson and a group of sober citizens by his side. His gaze struggled up through the flooding din to the tiny figures at its source.

"Young men!" he called in precise and ringing accents. They roared on, oblivious. He raised his voice. His words were smothered by the chattering jacks and the riveters' gross song. The position was ridiculous. Waving his fellow citizens to keep their places, he began, as majestically as possible, to climb the tall ladder to the tank.

The group at the base of the tower saw, against the sunset, the black and shapeless figure of Mr. Scabes slowly ascending the long steel web. As he mounted through the volume of harmony, his steps quickened until they were in time, and in time to a melody of no righteous import. He was seen to gain the summit. The music stopped. They saw six large, mechanics' hands reach down and haul him to safety. Mr. Scabes sat there silent, breathless no doubt. They saw the three pariahs steady him on his perch familiarly and point across the plain into the blazing West where the Blue Ridge rose, then eastward toward the sea, hid from the groundlings under the shoulder of the world. They saw Mr. Scabes stand up, holding by their arms and swing the compass round till his flat, old face glowed again in the flaming western fire. Waiting below, they felt the swift advance of twilight and the earth-creeping evening chill. And still Mr. Scabes did not speak, only stared into the heart of the distant light. At last they saw the four heads come together. The message was being given. Then upon their upturned faces descended a long "O-o-o-o-o-o-o-h, she-e-e ripped and she snorted and she rolled on the floor—"

They looked to see the apostle turn and strike the singers down. Instead he only stood there rapt and radiant, gazing into the eye of the sinking sun, gently swaying to the rhythm of their song.

The Verse on the Window

WEATHERBY HEATH pulled up the gray horse at the foot of the hill. He turned in the saddle and looked back at his old, rambling home. He looked ahead at the gleam of the James below the shadow of the bluffs. Taking off his gold-rimmed spectacles, he rubbed them reflectively. He was, in fact, pretending to debate where to ride that day.

"Well, come on, Bumper," he said. His ruddy face was touched with gentle self-ridicule. He started on a staid trot for the inn—just as usual.

Jogging along between the sagging weathered fences of the half-abandoned countryside, past the choked hedgerows, he thought how like that countryside he was. His life, once full of promise, still showed a certain beauty, but no one knew better than he that it was the beauty of frustration and decay.

His bright imagination was still gilded with romance, and he would in his day have made a tender lover. But he had been too shy to push his fortune with the undemonstrative, while the others filled him with terror, both for his person and for the fanciful ideals that blossomed in his heart. He had passed those years divided between discouragement and dread, until at last time gently withdrew him from the arena.

But there had been one moment—years ago, one moment only. She was a tall girl with a shy, reserved face; a girl who beckoned and fled. He had seen her twice—a naiad. "The Naiad—the Naiad!" he had said, and written a sonnet to her in one glowing hour. That very evening he had gone to her, and then, at the last, turned craven and mumbled conventionalities. He had crept home, loathing himself, the sonnet still in his pocket. It lay in his desk to this day—his one good thing. But she had married long ago; and he knew that if they ever met, her eyes would mock him.

"Come, Bumper," he said. "Don't go to sleep."

Bumper raised his muzzle from the road, trotted three steps and subsided. The horse, too, was getting old. Heath touched the white, woolly neck. Bumper and he—two old gray friars on their monastic hill; Bumper alone in the old stable, and he alone in the old house; the horse aging in merciful stupidity, and he in gentle anguish, the last Heath dying frustrate, unexpressed, sterile.

He had written much—historical studies, published through kindness, with no success. His modest books were of another age, an age as antique as their subjects; they were born old, as he perhaps had been. He still wrote, growing less hopeful and more industrious with the years; but he gained no recognition. He received friendly words and some encouragement, never homage. He had never written a line which reached its mark.

His days for love and writing were past; he knew it from the fact that he found solace in the minor affairs of life. It was one of these which drew him each day to the almost deserted inn. As he crested the hill he saw it, lonely, dejected, down at the heel, huddled beneath its oaks beside the crossroads. Beyond, a battered gold-and-scarlet sign, shining resplendent in the setting sun, announced some long-forgotten brew to travellers long forgotten.

Drawing nearer, Heath made out what he was searching for. One end of the inn was lighted by an ancient window of colonial design. Above it a round arch embraced a fluted shell, and on each side smaller panes spread their dim, delicate pattern. There was a place at "Brownheath" which that window was predestined to fill. But Heath was keenly aware of how great an affront such a proposal might be to the present proprietor of the inn. For this reason he had never so much as pulled up on one of his visits. Indeed he was covered with confusion whenever he felt that the landlord had observed him passing by.

To-night, however, the panes of the window glowed like rubies in the silver setting of the old white frame. The house was melting into the soft dusk. The window alone flamed out, lovely and desirable. Heath stopped the gray and looked at it intently.

The whole was very simple, yet its beautifully just proportions gave an effect of inevitability that delighted the heart of the eager, timid man on the wise, gray horse. It was like a verse of Burns.

" 'My love is like the red, red rose,' " he murmured to himself. He repeated the whole poem and looked at the window. The art of each was the same.

He was roused from his thoughts by the discovery that

Bumper had taken advantage of his abstraction to edge imperceptibly toward a withered rose bush and was nibbling it with satisfaction. He caught up the reins hastily, and at the same moment discovered that he was being observed in no friendly manner by the proprietor.

That wizened figure, with sharp, cool eyes and toothless, tucked-in mouth, was sitting perfectly lifeless on the porch and had undoubtedly been there from the first. He still made no sound, but he had turned his birdlike head and fixed on Heath a steady look of hostile indignation.

Heath sat motionless, deeply perturbed. He could by a little click of his tongue rouse Bumper and trot briskly out of his dilemma. But nothing was more impossible than to give that click. It would be shameful. He must stay and do the best he could. He made a hesitating gesture of salutation and said: "Good evening. Are you the proprietor?"

"That's right," the ancient replied in colorless tones.

"Well, I'm sorry about my horse. I never noticed."

"What about him?"

"Why, he started to eat your bush. But not very much."

Too late Weatherby realized that, after all, the trespass had not been seen.

And too late the aged landlord learned what a satisfying grievance had escaped him; he contented himself with a rasping sound of undetermined significance and a second grim stare.

"The fact is," murmured Heath diffidently, "I was looking at—at what a nice place you have here," he went on more boldly. He took a cautious glance at the acrid figure. "A nice place," he continued, "a very nice place."

Retreat was now impossible, and he proceeded to comment on the virtues of the inn. He took heart at the sound of his words; he warmed to his work; his gold-rimmed spectacles and kindly face twinkled with humorous enthusiasm that drew at length a reluctant cackle from his adversary.

" 'Tain't so bad," he said. "Come inside. Show ye round." He shuffled warily to his feet.

Heath patiently inspected the golden oak furnishings of the office, the bar of many mirrors and the horsehair parlor, with its nocturnal chromo in which the moon proved to be nothing less than an ingeniously arranged disk of genuine mother-of-pearl.

While he was still exclaiming over this the proprietor led him, apologetically, to the place of his desire.

It was a long room with a flat vaulted ceiling. At the far end the tracery of his window showed sharp in the evening light.

"Dusty, ain't it?" the cracked voice said. "Never used 'cep'n for dances. Looking at that old window, I see."

Heath faced him guiltily.

"Curious thing, that old window. Look at it close. See anything?" He came scuffling up to Weatherby and pointed a lean finger at the lower, left-hand pane.

Heath followed it and made out, scratched on the glass in an old style of hand, the words:

Phyllis, no more I worship at thy shrine.
Breathless, I wait no more upon a sign.
Proud and alone, wandering, wandering far—

That was all.

"Old writin'," the ancient explained sententiously. "Po'try. A fellow wrote that maybe a hundred years ago or so. They tell about him still. Young fellow, no 'count. A po't, said he was. Had some trouble with a girl or other; used to come in here to get drunk. This was the taproom then. One night the proprietor, named Grutch, caught him markin' the window. Made Grutch mad clear through; fine new window then. Here was this young feller, owed Grutch money, scratchin' the glass with a real diamond ring. Grutch started to cuss him and 'stead of apologizing the young fellow come at him with a sword like they all carried then. 'Blast you!' he says." The old man chuckled. " 'How dare you interrupt me?' That was the last he said, though. Grutch rapped him on the head with a fire tongs; that was the end of him. Po'ts is funny: there he was, hadn't paid his account—"

Heath was looking minutely at the writing. "By gracious! Pre-Revolutionary script," he murmured.

"Folks say he haunts the place," the toneless voice droned on. "Once a year—night he was killed, I s'pose they figger it. Anyhow they won't come here to dance that evenin'."

"I wonder why he comes back?"

"Well, it ain't to pay his bar account"—the old man gave a dry cough of mirth—"for I never seen him, and I been here thirty years come Christmas."

"I don't suppose you would like to sell this window?"

"Dunno as I mightn't, if I could get enough to put in a new one. This's all leaky round the sash."

The window was bought for a price, and Weatherby had it carried up the long drive to "Brownheath" and fitted into the living room. The room itself was well beamed and mellow; the graceful frame blended with its setting.

Meanwhile Heath returned to his work. He spent the autumn collecting material, and when winter came he settled down to write. And yet he did not wholly settle down. For as the days passed he found his thoughts returning to the window and the landlord's story. Bit by bit he reshaped every detail of that almost forgotten scene. He pictured the old taproom with oak tables curtained off by green baize. A roaring fire threw weaving lights and shadows on the flat vaulted ceiling. Knots of gross idlers clinked glasses in the dark recesses. At the far end the frosty moonlight streamed through the window and touched the pale, fine-drawn face of the wild young man.

Heath saw him, filled with wine and poetry, bending forward in his wide-skirted coat, scratching intently on the pane. He saw the stolid, surly landlord rudely break in upon him and the quick rush of Cavalier blood. He saw a sword, half-drawn perhaps, and then the blow.

Heath stirred the logs absently. How drab his own life had been. He almost envied the other—envied his last blazing moment of defiance. If failure were inevitable, as it would appear, among destiny's marked men, his was the way to fail. But that, too, seemed part of the doom. One could no more choose another's failure than another's success. He himself had not asked much of life. He would have been content if he had written only one good thing.

But had he not? He went to the desk and took out his sonnet, still in the envelope of that fatal, frustrate night, the night now so long distant, when he had stood, abject, in the dark wood of romance and watched the Naiad flee. The thought no longer thrust him through; it was only a memory now, sad, but shadowy.

He read the sonnet. It thrilled him still, thrilled him of

itself. What fire he must have had that day! There could be no mistake; this was poetry indeed. He could do nothing like that now. And when the end came he would go out, unexpressed, as had the pale young man. What was the need? Here was the sonnet. He had failed with it in love, failed irretrievably. But while there was time, why not wrest a victory from his defeat? The verse was really good; they would have to acknowledge it. They would see that he was not altogether futile, after all.

He could not, however, stoop to make capital of lost romance. He would prove his true worth only to himself.

He copied out the sonnet neatly. "Ad Solem" he called it, "by Icarus." He addressed it to *The Quarto,* where most of all they would know its worth.

An answer should have come back in a week, but it did not, although each day Heath rode Bumper to the post office, jogged down briskly in happy excitement, walked home slowly, deserted by fame and recaptured youth.

Yet he knew a letter would come, and even pictured to himself what it would say, pictured the editor's cordial surprise at the new planet that had swum into his ken. He had struck the true note; it was enough; one true note, ringing in the lonely hearts of men he should never know, ringing on, faint but still true, long after he was gone. One thing he determined: no matter how they importuned, he would never disclose his own name; he owed that to the Naiad; though perhaps she would mock him for his delicacy, as she would mock him for his cowardice. Nevertheless, he would go through to the end, proud and content, in secret glory.

In the evenings he sat before the fire, thinking of his

own life and the forgotten poet's, so different, so distant, yet doomed to frustration like his own. The romance of the dead youth touched him and shamed him. For the other had lost the prize through pride, perhaps, and circumstance, while he himself had been meanly balked by his own fluttering fears. The pale young man whom he could see stretched, face down, on the sanded taproom floor, and he himself, warming his felt slippers before the hickory blaze, both stood for lost romance.

The letter came to the post office. He thrust it in his pocket and cantered back through the shadows to the warm lights of his home. He opened a bottle of wine for dinner and sat musing in its warmth, touching the letter in his breast. He would open it after dinner.

In the living room he drew up to the fire and lit his pipe. He held the letter in his hand a little sadly. He had given them his best, and they could not deny him; but it was his best of long ago. He tore the envelope. There lay his sonnet and a little printed slip: "The Editors of *The Quarto* regret"—and so forth.

The clock ticked on and struck the quarters softly, but he did not stir, except, every so often, to refill his glass from the bottle beside him and then sit back again, looking into the fire.

He had brought them a gift from the inner sanctuary, and it did not move them.

He folded the copy neatly, finally, and, going slowly to his desk, he drew out the faded original. He patted it quietly as if to ease its pain, his hands shaking a little, then dropped both papers in the fire.

Outside, the night was harried by wandering gusts of wind. He glanced up at the window. The moonlight was flowing through the small, wavy panes, as he had pictured it in the taproom scene. He thought of the line:

Phyllis, no more I worship at thy shrine.

What else was to come? Defiance? Or had the proud and sensitive poet revolted from a mistress who used him ill—or too well? He would suffer for that, suffer more than death. The wind, in a last burst, died out. The world was suddenly still. The clock sounded like the beating of hammers through his whirling thoughts. He looked at it. It was almost ten.

He heard the garden gate click softly to, then what seemed like cautious footsteps crunching on the frosty gravel path. The front door, swinging open, let in a stealthy wisp of cold night air. He huddled nearer the fire and watched the door.

The portières swayed; a very slender shaft of light slid through the narrow opening. It paused as if in suspense. Heath saw that it was the blade of a sword.

The fire burned low, the curtains swung, and in the shadows it seemed as though a slim young man in old dress had stepped into the room. The face was dimly white. Only the eyes glowed with the somber light of other worlds. He appeared to look at Heath intently, his sword on guard, distrustful and confused. He gazed uncertainly about the room. Moving slightly among the moving shadows by the wall, he seemed to glide toward the window.

A wisp of cloud had turned the moonlight to a misty, silver gray. The form of the young man, melting in the moon dusk, appeared before the familiar pane. He bent over it, with a quick, certain gesture.

He seemed to sheathe his sword. His hands fluttered together. He was drawing off the ring.

The shadow slipped to the floor and busied itself at the pane, the dark head drooping low between the shoulders of the dark coat, the broad skirts swaying in the shifting eddies and wavering lights. He looked up apprehensively and saw that it was twelve minutes past the hour. Covering his face with his slim hands, he gently shook his head from side to side.

At the quarter a low whistle sounded from the foot of the hill. The young man sprang up, his face whiter, his eyes darker than before. He stretched his hands in supplication toward the pane. Again the distant whistle sounded. He unsheathed his sword and, turning with quiet swiftness, he slipped through lights and shadows and was gone. Outside the wind sprang up and drowned his hurrying steps.

Heath was already at the window. But saw only silver snow patches beneath the chilled half-moon. He lit a match and looked closely at the pane. It was unaltered:

Phyllis, no more I worship at thy shrine.
Breathless, I wait no more upon a sign.
Proud and alone, wandering, wandering far—

Heath read the lines again. The match went out. He stood in the dark where the murdered poet, straining to add another line, had knelt just now. Slowly he seemed to feel the lost words stir to life and form themselves in air out of the other's striving. That desperate labor had left no mark. Yet the poet's thoughts lingered in the room with all the fragrance of their first birth. So real the crowding couplets seemed that Heath was plucking at a diamond ring he wore. He closed his eyes. With a gentle shock the last line, lucid, flawless, complete, rang through him.

So it seemed at least. But he was overwrought . . . the wine, the vision, his distress . . . he shuddered in the cold and stumbled off to bed.

The next morning the fragments that had come to him did not appear in any way remarkable. Indeed, as time went on, the more he repeated them to himself, the less unusual they sounded. Though fond of poetry, he was not a poet; he was almost a failure as a writer of prose. He decided to suppress the whole affair.

But nearly a year later he found himself awaiting the exact date with some anticipation. He made sure that he would be alone. As the hour approached he darkened the room and sat by the fire. He knew now why the pale young man returned and always would return. There was a sonnet—he went to the shelf—yes. He sat down with the book.

Love is not love
Which alters when it alteration finds,
Or bends with the remover to remove:
O no; it is an ever-fixèd mark
That looks on tempests, and is never shaken;
It is the star to every wandering bark,

Whose worth's unknown, although his height be taken.
Love's not Time's fool, though rosy lips and cheeks
Within his bending sickle's compass come;
Love alters not with his brief hours and weeks,
But bears it out even to the edge of doom.

Heath closed the book and looked toward the window. There in the darkness was the poet's "ever-fixèd mark," the star which drew his wandering bark forever back to it. Where were the rosy lips and cheeks of Phyllis, long-forgotten? What matter?

Love alters not with his brief hours and weeks,
But bears it out even to the edge of doom.

Heath dropped his head. He knew now how great a thing his timid heart had shunned. For him romance was fled, and in that fire where his sonnet turned to ashes, fame was lost as well. No woman's heart would thrill for him, no reader pause to render him a silent salutation.

The garden gate clicked faintly in the distance. He was coming again.

Fumbling at his diamond ring, Heath stepped swiftly to the window. The missing lines came surging to him.

Phyllis, no more I worship at thy shrine.
Breathless, I wait no more upon a sign.
Proud and alone, wandering, wandering far—

he read, then wrote:

I seek new gods where fairer temples are.
Yet on what altar shall I pour my wine?
For every fane I enter seems like thine.

He went back to his chair, trembling because of what he had done. He heard the front door creak softly and felt the curtains sway. Not daring to look, he knew the youth with the sword had entered. He was in the room. He was looking at him. Heath raised his eyes. There stood the slim, dark shadow.

Now he seemed to be moving to the window, drawing off his ring. He stooped over to write—then started back. With one hand shading his eyes from the firelight, he bent over to read what Heath had written. He swept off his hat and dropped on one knee. His hands went out on either side to the slender frame. Leaning forward he pressed his lips against the pane. How long he remained thus Heath did not know.

At last the same low whistle again was heard. The young man sprang up, smiling tenderly. He looked Heath in the face and, placing his three-cornered hat over his heart, he made him a ceremonial bow.

Weatherby Heath felt his timid spirit give one great, fluttering leap of pride. He was on his feet, returning the other's salute.

A log blazed up. The room was empty.

The Gizzard of a Scientist

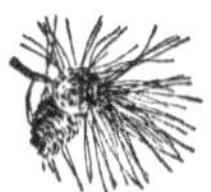

He leaned forward under the light and marked a cross on the frosting of the julep glass.

"If anything ever gets me," he said, "I reckon it'll be this."

Outside, the evening breeze off the harbor made the palmetto leaves in the garden clash together like light strips of wood.

"Well, if it don't," I said, "you're bound to be quite a doctor."

The breeze came in through the lattice and stirred gently, soft and warm.

"Yes," he said, "it'll be this. The women I can leave alone."

"You surely can," I said.

"Well, they've no complaint," he said. "They know me."

"Yes, I reckon they do."

He did not look pleased. His hair was coarse and bushy and his black eyes stared at the bottle, under bushy eyebrows. His nose was narrow and fine, but the rest of his face was blunt and his broad ruddy cheeks showed he came from back up in the State. Along the coast the men's faces are white and the more they drink the whiter they get.

He never was one of us. A coarse streak of the country man, a hard-bitten earnestness; and a way of saying the wrong thing. He knew he did it. But he didn't know how not to. And he didn't care. Not much anyhow. If he felt he was a little queerer than other people, he figured, too, that he was a lot more sane.

"It won't be the women," he said.

He stared at the bottle with a hand on his plain chin. "Southern chivalry," he said. "It don't fool me. It's just a high-toned grade of rootiness."

"Oh, go to hell, Rennie," I said. "You're a back-country man and always were. You don't know what it's all about."

"Don't I?" He looked at me and wiggled his eyebrows, very earnest and uncouth. "It's you sweet-scented cavaliers that are the suckers. Diddling around with your notes and flowers and valentine poems. And what do you all amount to?"

"Just a back-country Presbyterian," I said.

He pounded his glass on the table; ice tumbled down. "Women are for men who haven't anything else. I have."

"You have liquor," I said.

"I've got science." He looked in through the frosted glass as if he was reading something. "I've got the gizzard of a scientist and I know it," he said. "And women aren't in the picture."

"What about a woman?" I said.

He looked up, absent-minded and impatient, like a man who has been disturbed in his work. "It's all the same," he said.

"No," I said. "It's not."

He thought about it. They were my juleps and so he

had to consider what I said. "Oh, well," he said, "if a man wants a woman for intercourse, cooking, and children let him marry a farm girl like some of those French painters. Aught else just bothers his work."

"What about Madame Curie? Wasn't she a help to her husband?"

For the first time he looked pleased. "She surely was," he said. He stopped to give me a chance to look pleased myself. "And the help she was," he said, "proves what help he needed. A man don't need help."

"Rennie, talk sense," I said. "You know two heads are better than one."

"Not when it comes to thinking," he said. He stuck a square finger at me, as cocksure as a country preacher. "No two heads are better than Pasteur's," he said, "and they wouldn't be even if his was one of them."

"What about the woman who don't ask anything for herself, just worships the man?" I said.

He shook his head. He was sad and pitying. "That's bad."

"Well," I said, "you're bound to suit yourself, but it sounds like a lonely life to me."

"That's what it is," he said, "and that's the beauty of it." He was joyful. "Every man is alone in this world and the sooner he knows it, the better he is off."

"How about every woman?" I said.

"Oh," he said, "damn the women." He looked at the bottle. "This is surely good liquor."

"Jamaica rum makes a good julep," I said. "You don't have to put in hardly any sugar."

He finished the julep with his head back. A little piece

of ice fell on his face. He stood up, dusting at his linen suit with his hands.

"The tail end of a julep is never much," he said.

"That's a fact," I said.

"Just ice and water and mint," he said. "Those were good juleps, though." He studied about it. "The trouble with juleps is you always quit right at the tail end of one. The place to quit would be right after one swallow of a fresh julep."

"That's a fact." I admitted.

He shook his glass and made the ice rustle down. "A julep's an anticlimax."

"I'll wake up Cicero," I said, "and get more ice."

"No, we wouldn't do it," he said. "We'd go on to the tail end of that one. I would. And I've got patients to-morrow." He turned his square back and tramped out the door.

"I'll walk down to the gate with you," I said. I didn't want to say it, but he was a man you never treated as he deserved.

Outside, the palmettos made their rustle in the night air. Through the bars of the iron fence we could see the fixed light on the breakwater and the live oaks along the water front.

"You know, I don't like this place," he said. "The air is no good and the water is no good."

"How do you know about the water?" I said.

"I've washed in it," he said. "It don't even feel good."

"What did you settle down here for then?" I said.

He turned around in the dark and looked at me as though I lacked sense. "A man needs hospitals and plenty of niggers to work on. Up home everybody would be my friend. I couldn't try anything."

"Lord A'mighty," I said, "you don't need to try things. You know enough now."

"Brother," he seemed to be brooding over me, suddenly affectionate but still hopeless, like the father of an idiot child. "We don't know a thing," he said. "Not even the big fellows. Not yet. Bio-chemistry—" He turned the handle of the iron door. "Good night, Cass."

About a month later he telephoned me. "Come over to the place," he said. "We'll have some juleps."

It was only around the corner in a narrow street that led back from the harbor between high white walls and the ends of galleried houses. The street lamps, swaying in the regular night breeze, made black shadows of porches and lilac trees. His whitewashed house and office were the old slave quarters of the L'Estrange place and stood flush with the street. There was a carved brass knob on the blue door.

He had on a fresh linen suit and a bright blue tie. Right away, I knew by the way he talked that the juleps were not going to be a frolic.

"Come on in." He shut the door on the office side of the hall. It must be one of his scientific problems.

He opened the other door. I started for it, wishing there was some other place where we could sit. Rennie's notions of a parlor were pure back country—a couple of mail-order tapestry chairs, a frosted ceiling light and some hand-colored photographs in gold frames.

Under the light, looking straight ahead, sat a white-faced girl with soft black hair. My Lord, I thought, she's in trouble. But why me? And why Rennie? She couldn't have picked a worse bet. Maybe he expects me to fix her up with one of the other doctors. I got pretty sore. A fine occupation.

"This is my wife," Rennie said. I reckon he must have said it although it is one of those things that destroy themselves in the confusion that follows. I had, at one moment, a dim notion that he was being funny and I might have said something fatal. But he came into the room and I saw she was his wife. She half rose from her chair. She was soft and slim. Her black eyes, under her mist of black hair, looked at me with a sort of shy reverence. I felt like something between a royal personage and a damned fool. So just being a friend of Rennie's made me a prince of the blood? Her white dress was nice in a homemade way. She was a country girl but no idiot. Not with that pale, half-smiling mouth. I looked at Rennie. In his new suit he looked like a square, cast-iron man. He just stood there with his blunt hands curled under the edge of his coat and looked at her. Now and then he would twitch his earnest brows. He was not excited or shy or sentimental; he was just a country scientist in front of his great discovery.

I reckon I must have said something because she was speaking. "Yes, sir," she said, "we were married yesterday." I knew by her talk that she had been raised on an island plantation.

"Now," Rennie said, "what about the juleps? I owed it to you, Cass, to ask you here first after that last talk of ours."

"Maybe so," I said, "but what about the lady? You didn't owe it to her to ask me—"

The girl had sat back in the mail-order chair and was looking at us about equally distantly.

"Rennie was talking foolishness one night at my house," I said.

"No," Rennie said, "the principle remains. I'll get the glasses."

"I'll do it," she said. "I make a good julep." She had on a pair of small-town, white-kid shoes that bagged around the tops, but her ankles were slim and she walked like an Indian. Some of those run-down old island families surely hang on to their quality.

Rennie tramped out after her. I heard them pounding ice in a bag. Once I heard her laugh. Her laugh was hushed and much lower than her speech, though that was low, too.

Her heels tapped in the hall. She came in with sugar and the bottle and a bowl of mint on a tray.

"No," she said. "Much obliged. I can do it. Rennie's still cracking ice."

"Rennie surely kept close about you," I said. "I didn't know a thing about it till right now."

She sat down and looked away but her voice was tranquil. "Well, I only beat you myself by a day or two."

"Is that a fact?" I said. "Hadn't you even seen him before?"

"Oh, yes." Like country folks, she was surprised I didn't know about her. "He was coming out to look after my father until he died."

"Oh," I said, "I'm mighty sorry to hear about that."

"It was for the best," she said. "My father had a cancer. I dreaded it for him."

"Yes indeed," I said. "I know. I'm sorry I mentioned it."

"There is no harm done," she said. "Since he don't have to battle it more, I'm glad."

"I expect it was hard on your mother, though."

"She died when I was born."

"I declare, I seem only able to bring up sad things."

"They're not sad to me. I'm used to them."

"Well," I said, "you're happy now."

"You know," she said, "I never thought it would turn out like this."

I said nothing.

"Whenever I first saw him I had to tell myself that he surely had a girl in the city."

"If you'd come to me, I'd have relieved your mind," I said. "He's never looked at a girl, here or anywhere."

"Is that a fact?" She thought about it. "I don't know whether that would have relieved my mind or not, to know that."

"Well, your troubles are over," I said. "As soon as you get acquainted around town you'll find a mighty pleasant lot of folks."

"I dread that, though. I don't take to strangers."

"Well, anyhow," I said, "you needn't to worry about it. Rennie never was much to go around."

"I saw that when I went over his things. There's weeks of work on his clothes." She looked contented. "And some of the coats are burned with acid."

"That's where he spends his time. In that laboratory upstairs. He'd rather do that than go out anywhere at all."

"He says that's the one place I'm not to come. Anywhere but there."

"Bluebeard's wife," I said.

"Is that a fact?" She was vague about it.

Rennie came in with the glasses.

"Look at that ice," I said, "it's as fine and dry as feathers."

Rennie wiggled his eyebrows at the ice. "You can't have good juleps," he said, "without you have good ice." He was like that; he knew more than any man in the city unless it was old Judge Burgaw, and probably more than him, and yet he talked bad grammar. He pulled up a straight chair beside me and looked at his wife. A careful satisfied look as if he was just checking up on everything to prove that it was so. "You can make them," he paused as if he didn't know what name to call her, "—Cass and I will talk."

She sat dropping the Bourbon out of a teaspoon on the cane sugar and ice. When Rennie was speaking she looked up, from time to time, as though she wanted to make sure that he was getting along all right. After the julep, I said I had to go. She stood up and seemed surprised when I held out my hand. She let her hand lie limp in mine. It was firm and there was a callous on the heel, but it was soft and warm and, even lying limp, had more life to it than the hands of most of our own girls; about which I ought to know, I reckon. All the way back down the street I thought about her hand and her and Rennie. It surely takes a man who don't know a thing about women to pick a good one. I've noticed that.

Well, that was the last I ever did see of her. She kept at home for a couple of weeks, fixing up his things, I suppose, and satisfied with that. Then I heard that he had taken her to the hospital to have her tonsils out. I had to laugh. It was like Rennie not to rest while there was a scientific error in his neighborhood. But something went wrong; whether somebody made a mistake, I don't know. You never can find out from these hospitals. She was to have come home the next day—the operation was nothing—instead she died in the night, a hemorrhage, I reckon; all alone. It was a scientific error.

While I was wondering whether I had better not go around and call, Cicero came in the big room and said Mr. Rennie was on the 'phone.

"Rennie," I said when I got to the 'phone, "I certainly—"

"They buggered things up," he said, "completely. I'm having the funeral this evening at four. You come, but if any other folks want to, ask them not to." He hung up.

In the room where we had drunk the juleps the shutters were drawn; the table, set back against the wall, was covered with flowers; three men in black were near the door. At the other end, a plain coffin rested on a light nickel-plated carriage with rubber wheels. Two of the men were young with buttoned-up coats and little black bow ties; they were the undertaker's men and they just bowed. The other man, with a white lawn tie and a brush of pale-gray hair over light eyes, stepped up and took my hand.

"The Reverend Boyer, friend," he said. "I never did know the unfortunate deceased," he said, "nor even the good doctor, but she was of our denomination, Baptist.

"A saintly person, I understand," he said. "Mighty sad. God's will." He let go my hand and looked at the door. I heard Rennie coming down the stairs.

I dreaded to see him. I was ready for anything. But I

wasn't ready to see him unchanged. He came through the door in his linen suit and blue tie, as busy and eager as if he had a case on his hands. "Howdy, gentlemen, Reverend," he shook hands, quick and awkward, all around. "Boys, you got the hearse ready? All right then. Reverend, I reckon you can do your part at the burying ground." He turned to me, "We can all go in my car. Never mind the flowers," he said to the undertaker's men.

We heard the motor of the hearse and then the undertaker's men came back and wheeled the coffin out the door. Rennie followed right after them. He stood looking on with his square hands at the edge of his coat. They ran the coffin up to the back of the hearse, then they got on each side of it and took hold of the nickel rails it had. They began to lift. Suddenly they looked at each other across the coffin and one's mouth flew open as if he were going to say something. He shut it, though, and they rolled the coffin into the hearse and folded up the nickel carriage. Rennie climbed into his little old Ford sedan and we got in the other side, the Reverend in the middle, trying to keep his feet out of the gears.

On the way out no one spoke. The Reverend cleared his throat a couple of times and then thought better of it; and once Rennie blew his horn till one of the undertaker's men looked back from the front of the hearse; then he waved to him to drive faster.

Just before we got to the cemetery Rennie turned to me. "You know," he said, "the city ought to inspect these outhouses here where they haven't got the sewer yet."

Beyond the cypress and yew trees of the old family plots there was an open grave with an old Negro leaning on a shovel beside it. He took off his hat and laid the shovel down. Rennie walked up and looked in the grave. "That's all right," he said. He pulled a dollar bill out of his hip pocket and gave it to the Negro. "You can go."

The undertaker's men set up their little carriage and rolled the coffin to the edge of the grave. Two nickel posts had been set at the ends of a sort of web sling. With a quick lift they moved the coffin onto the sling. Then they straightened up, very respectful and proper, and stood for a moment.

"That's all right, boys," Rennie said. His voice sounded loud. One of them folded up the carriage and started back to the hearse with it. The other stepped up to one of the nickel posts. He gave the other one a quick look.

"All right, Reverend," Rennie said.

The preacher bowed his head and started on the burial service. I bowed mine, but after a while I looked up. The undertaker's man had turned a little knob on the nickel post and the coffin was slowly settling into the grave. The preacher's head was low and his eyes were closed, but Rennie's head was up; he seemed to be studying about the machinery that made the coffin go down so smooth and slow. The undertaker's man's head was bowed, too, but once under his thin black eyebrows I saw him sneak a glance at the other one who was standing at the back of the hearse. The one by the hearse was staring at Rennie and his mouth was open again.

"Amen," the preacher said.

Rennie fished a ten-dollar bill out of his hip pocket.

"Preacher," he said, "I'm much obliged."

"Why, Doctor," the Reverend said, "that's not necessary—any time will do."

"Better do it now," Rennie said, "because I'm going to ask you if you'd mind waiting a minute and ride back on the hearse. I've got to hurry home. Cass, I'll drop you by your house."

I really felt sorry for that old preacher.

Rennie swung the corners and blew his horn all the way through town. About twenty feet in front of my house he locked his wheels and stopped in a cloud of dust. I got out.

"Anything I can do, Rennie," I said, "you know—"

He turned toward me. "You know that talk we had at your house?"

"Oh, well," I said.

"I was wrong," he said. He hit the wheel with his fist. "I was wrong." Suddenly his eyes looked very dark and sunk back in his head. "I should have done it myself. Those jackleg hospital plumbers—" He stepped on the gas.

It was about five o'clock when we got back from the funeral and by eight I began to wonder whether I had not better go round to his house. Maybe he might even want to come back and stay at my place.

The night breeze was blowing and the street lamps were swinging and throwing their sharp shadows on the white, empty street.

There were no lights showing in his narrow-fronted house, but I stopped in front of the blue door. Was he in the house? Standing in front of the door, I felt that I ought to be able to tell. Then I felt that I could tell that he was there. Perhaps he had gone to bed. I ought not to knock then. I ought to go quietly away. But maybe he was still awake. Maybe, even, he was sitting alone in the dark house and had been sitting there since night. Or maybe—it would be like him—he was working in his laboratory in the upstairs back-room. That would surely be like him. I smiled. Then I stopped smiling. Bluebeard's room I had called it that one time I saw her.

On tiptoe I went up a narrow alleyway that ran beside the house, straddling the narrow gutter down the middle. In the dark of the alley I could see that the white doors of his garage were closed. He was in, then. And on the big jasmine bush that stood beside it, lay a narrow thread of light which must come from one of his back windows. He was up there, tinkering; probably the best thing he could do. Even so, it would do no harm just to let him know that I had come by.

"Rennie," I said.

The bar of light on the jasmine tree went out.

I passed beyond the end of the house and looked up at the windows. They were dark.

"Rennie." I stood in the alley listening. There was no sound. But he was there. "Oh, Rennie!"

He surely could have heard me that time; and that was all I wanted. Just to let him know. There was no use to tiptoe now. I walked down the alleyway and home.

I didn't hear anything from him next day, so that night I went back again. Fast low clouds were coming in from the sea. Through the holes, stars showed and then went out like signal lights. It was all going on up above, though. Down below there was no wind and it was hot.

The street makes a little bend before it comes to his house. I was almost on it before I saw two men in front of his window. They were huddled close and were trying to look in through the pane. Their shadows, thin and sharp and tangled together, ran way down the street and swayed. I stopped to see what they would do. They just stayed there, crouched with their faces close to the pane. Looking for something; or looking at something. I went ahead stepping soft. As if there was a secret in that street.

I was right behind them before they jumped up. They stood side by side in front of the window looking at me, both in black with black bow ties. I knew them then: the two undertaker's men.

"What are you looking at?" I said, and I expect I sounded rough.

They looked at each other. Then one said, "We were looking at the notice."

"What notice?" I said.

They moved apart. A white piece of paper showed in the window above Rennie's doctor's shingle. I went between them and looked at it. Something was written on it. But the street was too dark. I pulled out a match and lit it. The undertaker's men stood there, looking at each other and then at me. One of them had his mouth a little open. I held the match to the window and read:

"Will be absent from the city for a few days."

It hardly looked like his handwriting. I lit another match. I could see the reflection of the undertaker's men in the glass. They were watching me.

It was his writing: but not neat, a wavering scrawl. So he was really gone then. But why all the secrecy the night before? And was he gone? The match went out, but I kept peering through the windowpane as if that notice, or the room, his office, behind the drawn shade, might have something more to say.

Then I turned round.

"Did you want to see the doctor?" I said.

They moved together in front of me.

"No, sir."

"All right," I said. "The doctor will be back in a few days. Good night."

The one whose mouth was open turned to me. He shut his mouth.

"Mr. Cass," the other one said. "I don't want to say anything—" He pulled out a cigarette and rolled it in his white fingers.

"Well," I said, "What is it?"

"We were coming to see you," he nodded at the other one.

"What about?" I said.

He studied his cigarette.

"Well, this fellow and me—naturally we handle right many coffins. You know."

"Yes," I said, "I expect you do."

He tapped the cigarette on his thumbnail.

"Well, whenever you handle a coffin, there's a way it feels."

"Yes," I said, "I expect so."

He threw a quick look at the house.

"That coffin didn't feel that way."

"You mean it didn't feel right?"

"No, sir, I wouldn't say that. No, sir, I—" he was nudged by the other one. "Well, I expect we have to be going."

He raised his hat. The other one raised his. "Good night, Mr. Cass."

"Hold on," I said.

As they passed around the bend in the street they turned and looked back at me. I could hear their footfalls for a long time.

I still stood in front of the door. The wind was beginning to reach down lower. In dark gardens beyond the walls the palmettos gave a rustle now and then. You could just hear the automobiles and trolley cars uptown and see, above the roofs, the light from the movie houses. I got out a match and a cigarette so that if any one came by I would be lighting a cigarette and not standing there looking at the house. After a while I went down the alley way to see if the bar of light still lay against the jasmine bush. But there was no light there or in his windows and I went on past a wooden door in his backyard fence, to the garage. I lit a match and shaded it with my hand and when I put my eye to the crack beside the hinges I could make out the nickel headlight of his car. I threw the match down and went back to the corner of the house and listened. Then all of a sudden I was calling his name; over and over. My voice sounded loud and scared in that narrow alley. I kept my eyes on his back windows; though now I did not want to see anything there. Then my throat shut like a trap and I whirled.

He was right on top of me.

"Hello, Cass," he said in a kind of wheedling whisper. And I knew right then that he had meant to do something to me.

"Hello, Rennie," I said, watching him close. "How you making out?"

His face was dead white above a two days' stubble and his eyes were bright, and far away. He had on his white doctor's coat and over the front of it were big dark stains.

"Rennie," I said, and I whispered too, "what's the matter?"

"Boy," he said. "Don't bother me. You understand?" He took a step toward me and I stepped back. "I'm working night and day," he said. "Night and day. Don't bother me." He stepped through the gate as quick as a cat and closed it behind him. I heard him stumble on to the back steps.

I started to whisper, "Rennie!" But what if he heard me? What if he came back? The door closed behind him. I got out of the alleyway.

I woke up the next morning early. A thin, green summer dawn was at the windows and the birds were bustling around in the last coolness of the night. As I went by the dining room downstairs, I stopped and poured out a drink from the bottle of corn in the sideboard. That is something I rarely do before breakfast. Out in the street the liquor hit me in the middle with a kind of hard hot spasm. But by the time I had gotten to his house I felt all right.

In the daylight things seemed clearer and simpler. I figured that by now he ought to have passed out and that I could get down to business and sober him up. I hated to go in there by myself but I didn't want any one else to know. News travels fast around our town. Every one knew he drank but he was noted for holding his liquor. Certainly he had never been in any fix like this before. Well, he had to be taken care of and I was the man to do it. Only what about the undertaker's men? I felt the good of the liquor leave me. What had he been up to?

I just looked at the front of the house to make sure that nothing was changed and went down the alleyway. The first rays of the sun were overhead and all the birds had started singing. The air was dead still and you could hear one lone automobile horn way up town and a ship's bell in the harbor.

I pushed open the door in the whitewashed fence. The yard was long and narrow between white fences, with a pear tree at the far end and, near the kitchen, a new clothes line on new poles. She had bought that, I expect. The grass in the yard did not amount to much at best and near the house it was dug up in a half dozen shallow holes. They were fresh too. It was those holes that had caused him to stumble. But then, had he been drunk after all? And what were those holes doing? They were dug anywhere, and the earth from them was gone. I looked. There was nowhere in the yard where it had been put. And a man would not carry earth into his house. But some one had carried earth into this house. You could see the trail on the kitchen steps. Right then like a sort of dull explosion down in a mine, I knew everything that had happened and what I was going to see. But I could not go back. Maybe it was that early morning shot of corn that held me to it. I only wished I had brought my gun—that was all. Instead, I picked up a knot of pinewood as I went through the kitchen door.

The dishes were neat on the shelves. No one had eaten there since her last meal. In the dim parlor the flowers were withered on the table against the wall. On the floor were the tracks of the nickel carriage's rubber wheels. I stood at the foot of the narrow stair and listened. Then I unlocked the front door. The cool early light came in. You could hear the birds all over that part of town, where so many gardens are. I went up the carpeted staircase, stepping close to the wall. It was still dark up there. In front of me the laboratory door was a little open. Through the crack a white electric light was shining on bottles and globes of glass. I took a grip on the pine knot and pushed the door back with my other hand. As it swung, he came in view, slumped stiffly in a chair and whiter than any dead man ever was before. Around his left arm was a bandage and blood was drying on the floor. I pushed again on the door. From the bandage around his elbow a thin tube ran to a sheeted figure on the table, to the sharp white angle of a woman's arm. There was a drift of dark hair.

I went down the stairs. The sun was coming in and the white street looked pink below the fresh new sky.

Civic Crisis

I

THE row of stores stood sharp and rigid in the Autumn sun. Across the street, the yellow railroad station stuck up by itself, and the bright rails stretched away until they curved around the rows of dead stalks in a cotton field. At this end of the block, a sycamore cast twig-shaped shadows on an iron bench and on a rotund figure. The old black suit was tight and bulky and solemn except for a nickel shield cocked up on the vest above the paunch. It said "POLICE," and winked as it rose and fell with the thick breathing. Under the bottom of the vest, stubby hands were plunged into the waistband of the trousers; in one cheek a quid hung on center, then rotated again.

A red eye looked out over this cheek at the slow movement among the stores down the street; people drifting up and down, Negroes inching along, looking in the store windows or standing in rows of three or four along the curb. The red eye squinted up severely. Too many Negroes hanging around. Always made out they had some business here in town. They ought to buy their rations and get back across the tracks. One of these days he'd pop down on them.

Dogs were most too numerous, too, he reckoned. Right now he could count seven and a couple of foxhounds. Up at this end, Burley Pellew's pointer was on his hind legs, looking into the trash barrel in front of the Emporium. Tom, the black and white depot dog, and a big kind of bulldog-looking dog named Jumbo, came up to help look. Beyond the filling station, Lawyer Benbow got out of his sedan and went into The Four Square Pharmacy for his morning coke, leaving inside the car that little, fluffy white dog the Yankee woman he had married had brought with her. The peaked white face peered out from behind the glass and Jumbo and Tom and two yellow town dogs came up to look at him.

Down the street, among the people, came the leather jacket and hunting boots that Proc Slosson always wore. Proc marched along straight and chunky, and came on past the filling station and on up to the bench. He needed a shave but his cheeks looked red and healthy, and his black eyes were bright.

"Howdy, Mac," he said. "It's chilly."

"Sure is," Captain Mac said. "Set down, Proc." He heaved himself slightly to one side.

Proc sat down on the iron bench. "Fact," he said. "Frost in the hollow again last night. Me and Hugh Billy was out."

The Captain brought his quid to a slow halt and looked at him. "You all have a race?"

"Got up a nice race. Over in Bear Grass Bottom."

"Ain't catched him?"

"No. It was a heavy race though."

"How many dogs?"

"Nine. His and mine and Dancy's Walker dogs."

"Thought Dancy was at the foxhunters' trials."

"Got back last night. Ate a meal and taken his dogs out. There's a man that's doted on foxhunting."

"How'd he made out at the trials?"

Proc shot the leather cap back on his small round head. "God in the mountain, ain't you heard?" he said. "Ninth in the All-Age and Reserve on the bench."

"With Tennessee Sal?"

"Certainly with Tennessee Sal. You can't beat these Walkers for trial dogs. I'm a July man myself, you know that, but I'll admit it. Of course, for a sure-enough fox-race they ain't worth a—"

"Hold on, Proc." The Captain's hands inside his waist-band made a muffled gesture. "Don't talk like that around the police house. I don't mind, only it don't look right."

"What did I say? Tell me what did I say?"

"I knowed what you was going to say. Ain't I heard you talk about Walker dogs before?"

"What else can a man say about Walker dogs?"

"Not at the police house. Was she out last night?"

"Tennessee Sal? She's shut up. Should have been shut up at the trials. That's what helped her out, I reckon: other dogs couldn't get their mind on the race."

The Captain pursed his lips and studied. He heaved back with finality. "That's against the rules."

"They won't never do nothing against a Walker dog," Proc said. "But if it's a July or a Red-bone see how quick they rule them out. In the score they had her third in speed and driving. It was trailing that set her back. Even so, Esquire Barfoot offered her a service to his old Puzzler. He was a judge."

"To Puzzler," Captain Mac revolved the news. "Well,

damn me," he said, "ain't that something? What's Dancy got to pay?"

"Two pups."

"No cash money?"

"Says not."

"Looks like the Squire thought something of Sal."

Proc locked his leather cap down over his eyes. "Or else was drunk."

The Captain withdrew one finger from his waistband and waggled it. "Proc, you can't take it away from her. Ninth in the All-Age and going to old Puzzler. What dog of ours ever equalled that before?" He made a sweeping gesture which ended at the sight of a Negro, small and quick by nature, approaching slowly. His hand went back inside his waistband. "Come here, Eightball; what you doing up town?"

The Negro came on beaming, with ingratiating and circular movements of his flapping shoes. "Yes sir, Captain Mac. Howdy, Mister Proc. Mighty pretty day if a man likes cold weather."

The Captain settled himself severely and waited for an intestinal rumble to subside. "Eightball, what you doing uptown?" he said.

"Just prowling by, Captain, prowling by." He turned a foot edgewise and studiously inspected the sole. "Seems like I can't pacify my mind."

"You still fretting about last night?"

"Ain't fretting, just studying. Captain, you the Law, what can I do about that window sash? And my window glasses? Two glasses, one foot by two foots."

"Eightball, what ails you? What did I tell you last night?"

"Captain, I couldn't say."

"God damn! Now listen. I'm going to tell you one more time. Listen good now; you hear me? You got no case."

"Yes sir. . . . Captain, how much would that cost new now?"

"Proc," the Captain turned heavily on the bench, "how much you reckon it would cost? A window sash?"

"Dollar and a half. At the warehouse. Course if a man wants to go to the mill. . . . Saw Rance Tazey there last week."

"How's he doing?"

"Doing fine. Mill, too. Got thirty thousand feet of cypress from old man Barneycroft."

"What'd they pay?"

"Talk like it was twelve fourteen."

"Who's getting it out?"

"Old J. B. hisself."

"Well, that's a fair price."

They reflected on its fairness.

"Captain, if you had been there your own self would you have shot him with your pistol?"

The Captain roused himself irritably. "What's that? Eightball, you still here?"

"Yes, sir, Captain," Eightball beamed as if he was telling good news, and then turned solemn. "Would you have shot him?"

"If I'd hollered to him to stop and he'd kept on."

Eightball was overjoyed. "Hey, hey, when police holler, man better stop."

With an effort Captain Mac reached back and disclosed

the pearl handle of a pistol at the edge of his coat. "When I holler they better stop."

"You know me, Captain Mac, I ain't never going to run if I hear you holler."

"That's where you got sense."

"Plenty sense. Man want to get along with white folks, he better do like they say. Ain't I right, Captain?"

"You got that much sense anyhow."

"Yes sir. Got plenty. . . . Captain, don't it look like he ought to pay me though?"

With his hands still in his waistband the Captain wagged his elbows at Eightball severely. "I ain't going to tell it to you no more. You-got-no-case."

Eightball shook his head with mournful relish. "Ain't that bad news though? Got no case. Declare I don't see how that could be." He brightened. "It was only just good dusk when I come home last night. So I ain't looking for no light in the house. And my sister she ain't looking for me on account I got off early from the ice plant on account they ain't making so much ice on account—"

"Eightball, move along, I don't want to hear no more about it."

"Yes sir."

"Mr. Slosson here and me have got some business."

"Yes sir."

"How you reckon I'm going to police this town if I set here listening to every nigger that wants to tell me his troubles?"

"That's right, Captain. You a busy man."

"Certainly I'm busy. They ought to have another man on here. And the town could afford it well and easy." He looked down the street at the two yellow town dogs cautiously stalking the tomcat that belonged to the Dixie Café. The tom bowed up his big gray back and the town dogs looked down their noses and walked on by. Those worthless fycts. He'd have loved to see a sure-enough fuss between them and that tom. There was a murmur from Eightball in front of the bench. He turned his head. "What's that, Eightball?"

"I say if you had only been there your own self last night. Ay, Lord, when folks see that star on your galluses they know that's the Law. But how it was, was that even so, though I wasn't looking for no light, even so, I suspicioned that there might be something that I didn't know what it was. And so I crope up on the house, tip-tip-tip like this, Captain." Eightball crept along the edge of the road. "And whenever I come to the porch I went to my hands and knees, creep-creep."

"Damn, Eightball, get up off the sidewalk."

"Yes sir." He rose up smoothly into a crouch. "And when I get to the door, here's me, Captain, with my ear to the crack. And so then I set the door ajar easy but I don't go in, just stick my head in like a snapping turkle." Eightball's head shot out. "This way. In there it was dark. And still I don't say nothing. You know me, Captain, I'm a suspicious man. So then I strike a match and right then I heard my bed go blam-blam, my own bed, and I hear a woman's skirts go flutter out the back way. 'Hey-o there,' I say. 'What's going on?' I say, and just then I see him coming, pom-pom-pom. I hear him run into chairs and tables and hit my bed one more time, blam-blam, and then he light out through the window, wham, sash and all, wham . . . ting-ting-ting. Ay, God, I ought to have grabbed that nigger." Eightball looked mournfully into space.

"You better be satisfied," the Captain announced. "He's mean."

"Captain, I'd have worked on him like a monkey on a peanut."

"You hear that, Proc?" the Captain said. "Says he'd have worked on him like a monkey on a peanut."

"Well, then," Proc said, "why didn't he follow him?"

"Now you say something different, Mr. Proc," Eightball pointed out. "I started but I saw the blood."

"He bleed?"

"Ay, Lord." Eightball gathered himself. "And so I don't know what I'm going to found—out there in the dark. Like the rabbit. Rabbit stop under old dead pine. Limb off the tree fell near about on the top of him. 'Hey, hey,' rabbit say, 'can't trust the living; can't trust the dead.' Captain, that's me, look how that creeper done me; a dollar and a half."

Proc stood up and pushed his cap back on his head. "Mac, I got to go."

"Don't go," the Captain said. "Eightball, you talk too much. Proc, I never did hear how the trials come out. Except for Tennessee Sal. Who won?"

"A Big Stride dog from Surrey Junction."

"That's Walker blood, too. Sal goes back to Big Stride two ways. When does Dancy carry her up to old Puzzler?"

"Friday. He figures to go up on number four and come back on seventeen."

"That don't give him long at the Squire's."

"Two hours." Proc's chunky figure swung slowly away.

The Captain did some mental calculation. "Well, as the fellow says, that's close connections."

"But don't it look like he ought to pay me?" Eightball said.

"Who?"

"What right he got to jump out through my window?"

"God damn," the Captain said, "ain't I told you you got no case? Ten times I told you you ain't got no case. Now here is the law about it."

Eightball bowed his head and folded his hands across his stomach. "Yes, Captain. Please to explain the law."

The Captain cleared his throat. "Here it is then. Ain't your sister let him into the house?"

"So she say."

The Captain stuck a thumb in the armhole of his vest. "So how is there housebreaking?"

Eightball considered. "Ain't he broke up my house, Captain? Ain't that housebreaking?"

"Hell, no," the Captain said. "You can indict a man for breaking into a house. Can't indict him for breaking out."

"Yes, Captain." Eightball had a thought. "But then, too, ain't he carried on in my house?"

"Did he give your sister money?"

"Beulah Belle? What for, Captain?"

"Talk up, Eightball. Don't make out you don't know what I mean."

"Hey, hey, Captain, she don't go with him."

"How come her to let him in, then?"

"Sis Highpocket was there."

"Doggone me." The Captain roused himself. "That long, loose old Highpocket. Well, did he give her money?"

"Him? Why, Captain, you know he's on Relief. That Highpocket give *him* money."

"Be dogged. So he goes with Sis Highpocket. She'll ruin him, just like she did Honey Boy."

"Ruint now, Captain. She's hog-wild over that black boy. Give that pigmy all she got and then come creeping in my house with him and—"

"Eightball, hush, I'm tired of hearing it."

"Yes, Captain."

"How's Sis doing these days?"

"She got plenty money."

"You go round there, Eightball?"

"Me? Captain, I'm earnest; you know I don't fool with no such womens."

"Where was it I seen you coming out of Sadday night?"

"Sometimes I goes."

"What you have to pay?"

"Dollar. Dollar and a half. Dollar the leastest."

"Is that a fact?"

"Ay, Lord. She's high. Just like a giraffe, Captain."

"Well damn me, and so she gives money to him?"

"Like I told you, Captain. Don't it look like one of them ought to put out for my window sash?"

The Captain opened his mouth to roar but Eightball had gathered his coat around him spryly. "On my way, Captain, just like old Number Seven." He cocked his elbows. "Hoooo-hoooo! Bam-bam! Morrell-Greenville-Birmingham-Mobile . . . sha-sha-sha!" Working his arms like pistons and chugging peacefully, Eightball steamed off down the sidewalk, across the street, across the tracks and down the path through the scrub oak that went to Possum Bottom.

II

For some little time there was nothing in sight except Tom, the black and white station dog, and one of Doc Pegram's old beagles meeting each other as though for the first time. They approached stiff-legged, stood end to end, sniffed gingerly and stared off into space. Then the thin figure of M. M. Sooler came wavering up the street toward the Captain's iron bench. The Captain filled in the time by working a case knife out of his trouser pocket and a plug of Mail Pouch out of his hip pocket and carving himself a slice. "M. M.," he said, "set down. How you living?"

"Can't object." M. M. sat down. "How you making it? You hear about Dancy's Sal?"

"Proc told me."

"She was Ninth in the All-Age."

"Proc told me."

"Reserve on the Bench."

"He told me."

"In speed and driving they had her third."

"That's how I heard it."

"But they marked her down on trailing."

"I know that."

"Esquire Barfoot's going to put her to his old Puzzler. Old Puzzler won the Derby at the Nationals in '15."

"Hell, man, ain't I been here when the news come back from Nashville?" For a while they sat on the bench. The Captain's eye, still angry, roved down the street. Lawyer Benbow's sedan was still headed into the curb and the peaked-nosed, white face of the lawyer's wife's dog was still peering out from behind the glass. A row of Negroes at a respectful distance were staring at the dog, and the dog, with his fluffy pointed ears up and his little black eyes popping, was staring at the grocery tomcat. Those Negroes had been there a long time and not a one of them showed signs of moving. White folks had got used to the lawyer's wife's dog; but the Negroes never would.

A little bristle-headed white boy in old corduroy knickers and a khaki shirt came up the street and took his place at the end of the row of Negroes. After a long while he came on again, still looking back at the lawyer's wife's dog. When he got near the bench he halted and hung back and stood looking at the Captain the way he had at the dog.

The Captain waved a flipper. "Heyo, sonny, what ails you?"

"Mammy sent me for the police," the boy whispered.

"Move over, M. M.," the Captain said. "Let him come here. Now, buddy, I'm the police. You're Miz Roon's boy, Keats, I reckon."

"No, sir. Keats' the youngest. I'm By."

"Well, what's the trouble, By?"

"Mammy just been to the hog pen. The speckled boar's gone."

"Busted out?"

"No, sir," the boy's voice came to him. He started a loud singsong. "It's stout every place. Mammy says he's stole."

"All right, son, don't you fuss."

"Mammy says they's wagon tracks right alongside the pen. Says she heerd a wagon screeching last night."

"All right, By, you tell your Mammy not to fuss. Tell her not to tromp round the pen no more. I might want to look for tracks later. Here, you like wintergreen? Run along." Reflectively shooting the stick of wintergreen in and out of his pursed lips, By went down the street. The Captain raised a bellow. "Possum Belly! You Possum Belly, come here."

The little yellow Negro was serious and stout and walked as though he were trundling his stomach on a wheelbarrow.

"Coming, Captain Mac."

"What you doing uptown?"

Possum Belly smoothed down the front of his mustard-colored vest cautiously. "Just come by to git some gun-powder for my yard dog."

"You aim to shoot him?"

"No sir. Going to feed him up on it. He ain't so fierce like he used to be. Come creeping round my place at night and he just licks they hand."

"How much you going to feed him?"

"All what I got in this twist."

"Better not let him set near the stove then. Next news you know he'll blow the roof off."

"He don't never come in the house. Sleep in the yard."

"When you go across the tracks, see can you find out who stole Miz Roon's spotted boar."

"He stole?"

"Stole last night."

"Do my best, Captain, can't do more." The full seat of his trousers swung sedately as he walked away.

III

The Captain rolled around on the bench and fixed his eye on M. M.'s thin face. "M. M.," he said, "I always said Proc Slosson was a clever gentleman, but sometimes he surprises you, I declare. Tennessee Sal has brought credit to this town, more so than lots of folks I could name. And still, just because she's a Walker dog, Proc throws off on her like she was some sorry potlick slut."

"He don't claim she's a potlicker," M. M. said.

"Don't right out claim it, but that's the way he talks. And look at her. Only four years old. And already she's got to where Squire Barfoot hisself is begging for her for Old Puzzler hisself. How can any man—" A shadow fell across his feet. Damn! Even before he looked up he knew it was another Negro. "Well, Ben. What you want?"

The Negro, black and thin and nervous, stood with his hands inside the bib of his overalls. "Excuse me, Captain, but they been a fuss across the tracks."

The Captain breathed heavily and eyed Ben. He bulged out one cheek and chewed hard on his quid. "What kind of fuss?"

"Cutting fuss, Captain."

"Who was in it?"

"Well, sir, some say one thing and some another, but Angel Jim cut up mighty bad."

"Whereabouts?"

"On the neck."

"I mean where was he at?"

"Well, Captain, some say one thing and some say another."

"Where is he now?"

"Who, Captain?"

"Angel Jim."

"In the big road."

"Where in the big road?"

"Front of Sis Highpocket's."

"This fuss start in Sis Highpocket's?"

"No, sir, Captain. No sir. That's just where he is now."

"What's going on in Sis Highpocket's this time in the morning?"

"Captain, I told you."

"Is he dead?"

"No sir. Ain't dead so far. Course he might be dead."

"Don't you know if he's dead?"

"Captain, he was living when I left. You ask."

The Captain thought the whole thing over, sitting motionless. Then he roused himself for a clean-cut decision. "Well, I'll take a chance on you, Ben," he said.

"Yes sir, Captain. Thank you."

"Go by the drugstore and tell them I said to notify Doctor Pegram when he comes by would he please to go over across the tracks. If he wants any information I'll be right here."

The Captain took a brief hitch to his trousers. "M. M.," he said, "you can talk, but we going to see the day when Walker dogs will sweep the country."

"I ain't got a thing against Walker dogs myself."

"You don't sound like you was for them."

"As the fellow says, show me a good dog and I'll show you a good breed."

"How you going to get good dogs without you have a good breed?"

"How you going to get a good breed without you have a good dog?"

The Captain clamped his fists and looked at M. M.'s thin, patient, sorrowful face. Sometimes he'd almost sooner argue with Proc. "Listen to me, M. M. Let me ask you something: Tennessee Sal's going to Puzzler, ain't that right? Well then, wouldn't you or any foxhunter be glad to get you a pup from them two?"

"That's because they good dogs. I got to go."

"Hold on, M. M. Let me ask you—"

"My missus," said M. M. and moved off.

IV

It was getting right comfortable now, and the sun had brought out more folks on the street. He saw Sis Highpocket's red hat and purple dress in front of The Busy Bee. That sinful old slut. Beat all how she carried on and took in the money at her age. He remembered her, though, when she was a right good-looking woman. For a Negro. He was working in the lumber yard then. Hey, hey, those were foolish days. Didn't have all this responsibility to maintain then. That looked like a strange dog in town, 'way down the block. He shifted to see if he could make him out but just then the highway Negro with concrete poisoning came limping in his gunnysacks right in the way. When the Negro had moved to one side the dog was gone. Must have gone down the alley. Most probably a strange dog. Not a neighborhood dog. There went the preacher's collie after him. Probably a dog fight. He'd listen.

The sun was warming to it, sure enough. He leaned back on the bench. All these dogs in town ought to have licenses. That was the ordinance. Well, most of them did. Some of them anyhow. The doctor's beagles had, and that speckled dog that lived up on the hill, never could remember his name. That was three. Well, if anybody made a complaint he'd probably have to do something about it. He remembered a little hound he used to have. Jenny. A little blue-ticked gyp he'd found when he woke up one morning. Those were the days when he used to drink. Used to foxhunt, too. That Jenny was hell on a fox when they got close to one. A sure-enough ketch-dog. But no cold-trailer. Probably not a purebred. That M. M. Sooler and his notions. Any man not a born fool would give fifty dollars for a Tennessee Sal pup; right now. . . . He heard a low voice, "Captain," and opened his eyes. He clasped his hands across in front of himself severely.

"Eightball, ain't I told you to go over across the tracks?"

Eightball agreed warmly. "Captain, I been across the tracks. Come back again."

"What for?"

"See could I speak with you, Captain."

"Eightball, I ain't going to listen."

"Captain, look what I got." Eightball wrestled a fist out of his coat pocket and opened it up slowly.

The Captain grunted. "Be dogged. Dollar and a half. Sis Highpocket give it to you?"

"Sis give it to him and so I got it."

The Captain nodded impressively. "You see that? You do like I say and you'll be all right. Ain't that right?"

"Sure is, Captain." Eightball answered mechanically.

The Captain cleared his throat and set himself to drive the lesson home. "If some of those niggers across the tracks could get that into their heads it would save them trouble. Plenty. You hear me?"

"Yes, Captain."

"You ain't listening. What you looking at?"

"Town dogs mighty oneasy. They goes three more."

"Where's that?"

"Down by the freight house. The doctor's beagles and old Grizzly."

"Whereabouts?"

"They gone, Captain, down the alley. Here come Tom, the depot dog, though, and Miz Roon's poodle."

The Captain raised his hoarse thick voice. "Here, Tom . . . here, Poodle!"

"Name, Wooly; that poodle," Eightball suggested. "But he ain't going to pay no mind now. Look at him sniff and lash his little tail. Poodle, your notion is the biggest thing about you."

"What's that?"

"Reckon Mr. Dancy's gyp mought have passed that way."

"Tennessee Sal? What you talking about, Eightball? She's shut up."

"Captain, I seen her just now. Down the alley. I was— Hold on, Captain—"

The Captain, running light and high, was hollering over his shoulder.

"Damn you, Eightball, you stay with me," he snapped his head around and kept on roaring. "Hey, Proc, grab that poodle. Hey, M. M., Pete, you niggers, grab Tom. Down the alley. Hey, fellows, come on, she's loose, Tennessee Sal. Hotter than—excuse me, lady. You, there, cut in the back way, God damn, don't stand there; there she goes! Jesus God, who let that poodle loose? Turn her, turn her, hold back them dogs, catch up that poodle. Can't nobody catch him? Shoot the pink-eyed little son of a bitch. Here he comes, close in, boys! That's good, Joe, kick him again. Here, little lady, here, Sal, now then, poor Sal, ain't nobody going to hurt you. You poodle, I'll cut your heart out. Eightball, get a rope, you hear me?"

The Captain breathed hard out of a corner of his mouth and ran his sleeve across his face. "Gentlemen, I'm much obliged. You know what that Eightball done just now. Stood talking to me for ten minutes and never said a word about it that this dog was loose. Good gal, Sal. God damn, a few months on the roads wouldn't do that nigger a bit of harm. Excuse my language, Miz Roon, didn't notice you was there, Ma'am."

Mrs. Roon bridled in and rared back until her front stood out like a corset advertisement. There was a cold look in her china eyes. "That's perfectly all right, Captain MacNutt," a smile froze on her thin mouth. "But what was that you said about shooting my Wooly?"

The Captain scarcely hung fire at all. "What, lady, shoot that pretty little poodle? Maybe somebody hollered it but it wasn't me." He got official and firm. "No ma'm, you ever hear anybody talk like that and you just report them to me. Shoot Wooly!" He laughed derisively and turned earnest. "Even if he ain't got no dog license."

From beyond the grinning ring there came a small dry voice: "Hey, Mac, ain't got no marriage license neither."

The Captain wheeled. "Who said that?" He drew down his mouth. "You-all better remember that there is ladies present. Proc," he said, "you carry Sal out to Dancy's." He turned benign. "M. M., just help Miz Roon with that little poodle," he said. "He keeps trying to jump out of her arms."

Fiesta

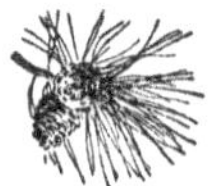

DOWN in the town, where red tiles and white walls showed among the cottonwoods, you could hear the drums and the tinkle of a Mexican band. Here, under the intense deep sky, the adobe courtyard stood out in the light. Everything stood sharp and unwavering. The light was cool and fierce and dry. Beyond the adobe wall, motor cars went by and three brown shining Harvey buses coming up from the main line of the Santa Fe. The road was a streak of humming that led to the big hum in the town. It was going to be quite a fiesta.

Through the open window, the office where Ed Chestnut was making up the weekly bills looked as black as a coal hole, except for the highlights on the typewriter and on Ed's bald head. He was typewriting with one finger; he had his pipe in the other hand.

"Say," he said, "you going to the fiesta?"

"What do you reckon I came down from Mora for?" I said.

"All right," Ed said without looking up. "Where do they have the 'and so forth' mark on these things?"

"What do you think I've got these new Pendleton boots on for?" I said.

"All right," he said. "Say, I've got another guest, a lady. She wants to see the fiesta. Be all right if she went with you? All right. Mother! Tell that lady it's all right. Tell her to get her things on. Tell her to hurry up."

He looked up at the paper in the typewriter roll to see how he was hitting it. "And say," he said, "if you go by the hardware store, tell them that oil stove leaks and where are those pump washers." He put his pipe in his mouth and went back to typewriting.

She was stout in her little old blue coat and her face under her blue hat was stout and pale. Her light hair was pulled back neatly. She got in and shut the door carefully. Then she tried it to make sure. She held her light blue eyes straight ahead. You could hardly see the lashes, they were so pale.

We rattled over the cattle guard. The road, black and shiny in the light, dipped away in waves over the gray mesa. The ruddy mountains rimmed us around and, down below, the pale green cottonwoods of the town clustered close in the gray desert.

All down the slope, she kept her hands curled carefully in her lap, holding onto her black leather pocketbook. She looked ahead at the adobe roofs and the cathedral towers above the trees.

"Well," I said, "it looks as if it was going to be quite a fiesta."

"Is that a fact?" Her voice was breathless.

"I've just come down for it myself," I said. "From Mora. I always stay at Ed's. Have you ever been in Santa Fe before?"

"Oh, no," she said.

"That's the cathedral down there, those two stone towers."

We came to the filling station—the first lines of brown close-built adobe houses.

"All Mexicans in this part," I told her. "The artists live up there on the Loma."

In the narrow street, we crawled along. Mexican children stood in the bright painted doorways and watched the traffic. We passed the thick adobe walls of San Raphael.

"That's San Raphael," I told her. "It's supposed to be the oldest church in the United States."

Each time I pointed something out, she looked at it seriously.

We rose up over the humpy bridge where the cottonwoods were turning a little yellow along the river. Then we went along the high Catholic brick wall and found a place to park by the side of the cathedral, between two buttresses. We walked around the corner and came out on the terrace. Between the rows of monks in brown cassocks standing under the trees along the terrace edge we could see the wide street across the front of the cathedral, filled with booths and hung with red and yellow bunting. Mexican families were eating on wooden benches; there were guitars and accordions and high harsh singing. From the plaza down the street, we could hear more music.

She stopped at the top of the terrace steps and stood looking down at the scene, with the adobe post office and the porch of the long low Governor's Palace beyond.

"I think I'll go back to Ed's about ten o'clock," I said. "Will that suit you all right?"

She nodded.

"This street goes down to the plaza, down there, where all the excitement's going on," I said. "The Trading Post is over there; you know: concha belts and blankets. And that's La Fonda, if you want to rest or anything."

She nodded again.

"You can get supper there," I said, "but the chili's better at Ernie's or any of the small places."

She nodded again and smiled this time. "I'll find a place," she said.

"You can ask anybody," I said, "except they're liable to be drunk. Don't ask Indians unless you want them to go along with you."

"I guess I can find a place myself," she said.

"I'll pick you up here," I said. The last I saw of her she was still standing there on the edge of the terrace.

In the plaza down the street a band was playing in the bandstand and a big slow mob was wading through the children on the grass. There were mantillas and high combs and a good many silver-braided wide straw hats and bright serapes. There were cow hands in store suits and Spanish heels, and artists in silver spurs and old Mexicans in frock coats, ranchers in tight Pendletons, and Indian school boys in belted jackets and little bow ties. Around the edge, Pueblo Indians in bright headbands squatted against the walls with turquoises and black pottery in their hands. Their braids were clubbed up with red worsted behind their heads. There were a few squaws, too. Their straight black hair and black belted dresses above white deerskin boots made them look square and heavy until they moved, and then they were lighter and stronger and smoother than American women. They kept their eyes down; their faces never changed.

I ran into some fellows and we went to a place we knew and had enchiladas and some Taos rye. It was a little patio with tables under a pepper tree. When the sun went down they lit candles and Mexicans came in to play and sing. It must have been nine o'clock when we left there.

Outside, the plaza was beginning to boil; noise and lights and music and gasoline flares and, on the house roofs and along the walls, candles glowing inside paper bags. They'd lit a bonfire somewhere and the piñon smoke made the air blue and smelled like incense.

In one corner a crowd was watching a platform where dancers from Old Mexico were working on the castinets. A Punch and Judy show was squeaking and under the porch of the Governor's Palace some Pueblo Indians had started drumming again. Other Indians and white people were forming around the drums. They called to us and we crowded in. Soon we had a solid ball, all holding to each others' arms and moving around the drum, tramping sidewise slowly and singing. People kept coming and joining, boys from the Indian School and white people in costume and a few Mexicans; there must have been two hundred, a big ball of people slowly moving around the drum.

Under the porch the drum echoed and the voices of the Indians around it would rise together to a high whine and then sink down, gruff and short. And underneath there was the shift-shift of the feet on the clay floor. In a tight mass, everyone shifted sidewise together around the drum. That was going around, too.

In the middle, you could see the faces of the Indians, fat

and shining and happy; their mouths open, singing hard, with a little smile at the corners. The drumstick flew up fast and the sound of the drumming filled the porch. Eyah-ha .... eyah-ha-ha .... eyah-ha .... eyah-ha-ha .... ee-aie .... haiee .... eyo-ho. There were no words, but they always sang the song the same, over and over. They were the best sounds for making each note.

"Heh." They sang it short with a droop at the end and stopped. Everyone stood still, looking at each other and grinning.

We crowded around. Under the lights the crowd was drifting and flowing. There were guitars and mandolins; a bunch would form and there would be that harsh Mexican singing. Lots of girls walked, two and two, in mantillas and old satin evening dresses, bright pink and yellow and pale green, or white. A couple of cow hands were drunk and quarrelsome and quite a few Mexicans drunk and affectionate.

Up by the cathedral, in front of the gasoline torches of the booths, two long lines of old Mexican men and women were dancing, balancing with short steps and whirling each other around, all very neat and clean and happy. They saw us and pointed to some Mexican girls who looked down at the ground and giggled. My girl looked like a square little shetland pony. She was light as a cat and when I made a mistake she laughed inside herself and shook her black hair.

On the high cathedral steps a monk in a brown cassock grinned down at us. He held the end of the rope that went around his waist and swung it in time to the music. Beside the steps there was a gold-crowned Virgin in a shrine made of piñon boughs; two brown old men in white cotton trousers were guarding it with guns.

Suddenly I thought about my lady. It must be eleven o'clock by now. Then I saw her. She was up on the terrace of the cathedral where I had left her. She was watching the dancing, following it, her head turning from side to side, not to miss anything. The light of the gasoline flares shone on her little pale plump face.

The music swung into the last bars and we all did a long whirl and stopped. As I got near her, the monk came down the steps and smiled and said something and she nodded her head hard. She was swinging her pocketbook in one hand and she had a package in the other.

"My lord," I said, "I'm afraid I kept you waiting."

"Oh, no," she said. "Is it time to go?"

"Well, it's getting on," I said. "Of course, they'll keep going all night."

She trotted behind me and climbed in the car.

"Did you see everything?" I said.

"Yes," she said, "I saw it all." She tried the door to make sure it was shut.

We passed the arc light on the bridge and the dark cottonwoods. The motor ran quietly in the night air. Behind us, we could still hear the fiesta. I looked back at the glow against the sky.

"Well," I said, "how was it?"

"It was worth it."

"Worth the trip?"

"Oh, yes," she said. "But it was a long trip. I came from Georgia."

"From Georgia?"

"Yes, Verney Springs. I teach school there. I've taught school there all my life." She held in and then burst out; her voice was sweet and strong. "Everyone said I was crazy."

"To come out here?"

"Yes; all except my sister. She said everyone ought to do one crazy thing a year."

"She sounds as if she had sense."

"Oh, she has. But even she wouldn't have liked it if I hadn't made up a story. Because I really only had enough for a round-trip ticket as far as Trinidad. I had to hitch-hike from there."

"Weren't you nervous, all alone?"

"Yes. Well, now I've seen it." She kept looking back at the glow over the town.

"Well," I said, "that was a tough trip just for the fiesta."

"Oh, no. It was worth it," she said.

"Is that so?"

"Yes." Her voice sounded pretty. "My father was out here when he was young."

"Is that a fact?" I said.

"It was in the old days." She was talking fast. "He was a young man. Then he came back East and married. He died when I was twelve. That was long ago. He used to tell me about it."

"Well, this used to be a pretty tough old town, I guess," I said. "In the old days . . ."

She was breathless. "He was a deputy," she said. "He shot two men. They were bad men."

"Is that a fact?" I said. "A real old-timer. Well, times have certainly changed. It's a pretty orderly town now."

"But it's beautiful." She tried to think how to say something more. "It's beautiful," she said.

The rails of the cattle guard rattled as we drove in the gate. There was a light in Ed's office and Ed was in there thumping away at the typewriter. I stopped the car and she got out.

"What's in the box?" I said.

"Oh," she said. "It's a belt."

"Concha?" I said.

"A concha belt. A silver one."

"Thought you'd run out of cash," I said.

"Oh, I kept a little. Just in case. I've got my ticket."

The light from the window fell on her face. You couldn't tell how old she was.

She was looking back at the shrouded town and the glow of the fiesta under the stars. The breeze brought a smell of piñon smoke.

"It's for next year," she said. "Next year when I come I'm going to have a costume."

www.ingramcontent.com/pod-product-compliance
Lightning Source LLC
Chambersburg PA
CBHW051924110726
47902CB00002B/404